"The cavalry has arrived."

Adding to her sarcastic comment, she looked at him as if he was the last person she wanted to see.

Didn't she realize a man had nearly choked her and shoved her back into a tree hard enough to break her? He stepped closer. "Are you okay?"

She waved a hand, anger darkening her eyes. "I'm fine. Now, if you're done playing the hero, I'm going to finish my run." She started past Lucas with nonchalance, as if some assailant hadn't just thrown her around like a rag doll.

He stepped into her path, his arms crossed over his chest. "You can't pretend nothing happened here. The police are on their way."

Everything about her hardened, from her expression to her posture. "You had no right to call them."

Something flittered across his flesh, a chill, an instinct. Whatever he called it, it was what had kept him alive in the desert.

This woman was hiding something.

And he had to find out...before it got her killed.

Jodie Bailey writes novels about freedom and the heroes who fight for it. Her novel *Crossfire* won a 2015 RT Reviewers' Choice Best Book Award. She is convinced a camping trip to the beach with her family, a good cup of coffee and a great book can cure all ills. Jodie lives in North Carolina with her husband, her daughter and two dogs.

Books by Jodie Bailey

Love Inspired Suspense

Freefall
Crossfire
Smokescreen
Compromised Identity
Breach of Trust
Dead Run

DEAD RUN

JODIE BAILEY

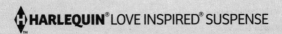

Recycling programs for this product may not exist in your area.

 LOVE INSPIRED BOOKS

ISBN-13: 978-0-373-45684-0

Dead Run

Copyright © 2017 by Jodie Bailey

www.Harlequin.com

Printed in U.S.A.

I have told you these things, so that in me you may have peace. In this world you will have trouble. But take heart! I have overcome the world.
—John 16:33

To my brother Matt, my first best friend.

ONE

Kristin James jumped sideways, one foot sliding on the gray dirt as she tried to catch her footing on the rough running trail around Smith Lake on the outskirts of Fort Bragg. "For real?" She threw up her hands, but the mountain biker blasted past, nearly driving her into the woods.

The rider didn't acknowledge her as he rounded the bend ahead and kept going, the whir of his tires fading among the pine trees.

"Share the road!" She yelled one more angry rebuke for good measure. *Seriously.*

Rotating her foot to make sure her ankle wasn't twisted, she stepped onto the trail and picked up speed again, the adrenaline from her near miss amping her heart rate better than the first mile of her run already had.

The All-American Marathon was the next month, and if she was going to maintain her time, she'd better push her training until the runners hit the start line in downtown Fayetteville.

And hope nobody else burst out of the thick pine trees to run her over.

The early-morning Carolina breeze whispered in the pines, mild for March but more bearable than the summer. Other than her "friend" on the mountain bike, she hadn't seen another soul on the trail. Exactly how she liked it.

A cracking noise around a curve ahead slowed her pace, and she wrinkled her forehead, her steps slowing.

The mountain biker roared around the curve, heading directly toward her.

What was he thinking?

The rider, his face covered by a gray ski mask, ground into the brakes as he neared, the rear end of the bike skidding sideways. The motion threw dirt and gravel on Kristin as she stumbled backward. Taking advantage of her unsteadiness, the rider reached out and shoved her out of the way.

Kristin fought to recover but fell hard to one knee, sticks and pine straw shredding into her skin. She scrambled to her feet and stalked toward the daredevil, who'd dropped the bike in the middle of the trail and stood eyeing her like he was ready for whatever challenge she threw at him.

Well, he'd gotten a bigger challenge than he'd anticipated. Kristin skirted the discarded bike and stopped arm's length away, sizing up her adversary. He wasn't much taller than she was, likely a gym rat, the kind of guy who wanted everybody to know his workout routine and to marvel at how he'd built a body by weight machine. He probably skipped leg day, too.

He wore gray cargo shorts, an odd choice for a mountain biker. A tattooed snake wound around his leg from ankle to knee, fangs bared and dripping vivid red blood.

Yeah, leg day wasn't this guy's favorite, and he tried to cover it with the scary tat. Nice.

If she'd had a card with her, she'd have flicked it in his face and told him what a good personal trainer could do for him. On second thought, she'd never liked his type as a client. Especially not since he was cocky enough to think running a woman off the trail was a viable way to get her attention. "What is your problem?"

A slow grin tipped the corner of his mouth, but it wasn't amusement flickering in his eyes. It was more like…determination. "No problem. Least not for me."

The way he said the words jangled memories in a pulse straight to her feet, driving her backward.

No. Kristin retreated from no man. Instead, she squared her shoulders, taking the offensive. "Watch where you're going. And don't come near me again."

She stepped over the rear tire of his bike and moved to start running again.

A heavy arm hooked around her waist and jerked her backward against a chest as hard as steel, lifting her off the ground. A beefy hand clamped over her mouth, twisting her head painfully to the side.

Kristin fought a rising panic. No one had laid a hand on her in years, but the memory bit, drawing long-buried fear with it.

He's not my father.

But he likely had more nefarious intentions than knocking any supposed disrespect out of her.

This kind of thing didn't happen to her. It just didn't. She was the one who taught women how to bring their inner strength out. She wasn't the one who was attacked on an early-morning trail run, a statistic for the six o'clock news.

Kristin tried to pull away, but the way he'd twisted her head to the side strained her neck and made movement virtually impossible.

Hot breath grazed her ear. "You scream and I'll make sure you never make another sound again. We're going to talk about your brother, Kyle, whether you like it or not." He jerked harder, and her neck screamed in protest.

Her brother? Kyle had been dead for months, killed by a sniper in Iraq. Given their years of estrangement and her brother's sorry track record for communicating, she would be the last one to have answers anyway.

Kristin scrambled for a plan, a way out. She dropped her struggle and went limp, judging his hold. What weapons did she have left on her body? She couldn't reach his instep or his throat…none of the vulnerable spots she'd learned in self-defense classes. And if she fought too hard from her current position, the likelihood of him breaking her neck was high.

There was one option.

With all of her remaining strength, she bent her leg and drove her heel back, catching her captor in the knee. The drive caught solid bone, and he roared, his hold releasing as he regrouped.

Kristin's feet thudded onto the ground, and one skipped out from under her on loose pine needles, driving her to the dirt. She ought to run, but if he pursued on the bike, she'd never be able to get far.

No, she had to fight. Turning on him, she balled her fists and prepared to throw every weapon in her arsenal.

He charged and drove her into a tree, the rough bark digging at her shoulder blade through her thin running shirt.

It took a moment to absorb the blow, but Kristin

fought, swinging her hands between his to break his hold. She landed on her feet and advanced as he staggered, driving the heel of her hand into his nose.

There was a thud, and blood soaked the gray ski mask.

The murderous intent vanished as he stumbled and cupped his face, pain erasing his anger. With one more look, he fled, running for the head of the trail with Kristin in pursuit.

Until the sound of running feet from behind had her whirling around to face the next attacker.

Sergeant First Class Lucas Murphy picked up speed, and his running shoes slipped on loose pine needles, threatening to take him down. He'd come around a corner in the trail in time to see a man shove a woman against a tree…and in time to see her school him in the finer points of self-defense.

Behind him, Travis Heath ran close on his heels. "You take the guy. I'll check on the woman." He hooked a left toward the woman and let Lucas pass.

Lucas pushed on, fighting to keep the fleeing man in sight as he cut through trees toward the parking lot. He couldn't overcome the head start, though, and stopped, helpless, at the edge of the woods as a red pickup spit dirt and roared toward the main road.

Adrenaline and the sudden stop forced his lungs to heave oxygen. His heart pounded from exertion and frustration. With his training, he should have been able to catch a hurting unit like the one the woman on the trail had sent packing. Even from a distance, it was clear her counterattack had the guy running in pain.

That took a special kind of moxie.

He fired off a quick call to the military police to report the incident, then turned and jogged through the trees, eager to meet the woman who'd fended off a man almost twice her size.

Although he was pretty sure he already knew her.

"I said I'm fine." The woman's shout bounced off the trees. If she was still in fight mode, she might be giving Travis a hard time.

Despite the seriousness of what he'd witnessed, Lucas couldn't help but grin as he scrambled over a tree trunk. If a woman came at Travis, he wouldn't fight her. And the beating a woman who could fight like this one would give him would be worth quite a bit of laughter at his buddy's expense if any of the guys in the battalion ever found out about it.

Sure enough, when Lucas broke through the trees to the trail, Travis was standing about ten feet from the woman, both hands in the air. "I promise we're the good guys."

"Then stand down and prove it." Her back was to Lucas, but he'd know her anywhere. Her chin-length dark hair was held back in a headband, and the way she'd planted her hands on her hips was a familiar stance whenever she wanted to assert authority.

"Kristin?"

Kristin James whipped around like she was ready to fight again, but her posture sagged when she recognized him. Those eyes, so blue they were shocking under her dark hair, caught his.

They never failed to stop him dead whenever he saw them. Lucas had moved in across the street from her in Haymount two months ago, after his last deployment ended. Unable to live on base because of his rank, he'd been thrilled to find the older two-bedroom rental off Bragg Boulevard. The place needed a little work, but it kept him busy. After Kristin kicked his rear in a half marathon the week after he moved in, they'd started running together in the mornings.

Kristin appeared more than a little relieved. "The cavalry. What are you doing here? And who's this guy?" She jerked a thumb over her shoulder at Travis, who acted like he'd walked into the middle of an absurd comedy.

Lucas couldn't blame him. There was something seriously strange about a woman who could face what Kristin had and then act like this meeting was a friendly encounter on her morning run. Must be a coping mechanism.

If it helped her to play this game, he would, too, at least until the police arrived and took over. "My buddy Travis. We were getting a run in before the duty day starts." The whole encounter felt stilted. He couldn't do it. After seeing the way she'd been shoved into a tree, he couldn't pretend life was sunshine and roses, even if that was her way of dealing. He dropped the charade and edged toward her, heel sinking in loose dirt on the edge of the trail. "Are you okay? He got a pretty good shot in before—"

"I'm fine." She bit the words into two bitter halves. Shaking her head like a mosquito was buzzing her, Kristin inhaled and her face settled into some weird, unnatural calm. "If you two are done playing the hero types, I'm going to finish my run. I've got three personal training clients today. I'll see you later." She started to move past Lucas with a nonchalance that couldn't possibly be real, as though some stranger hadn't thrown her around like a rag doll. The rough treatment was bound to hurt, but he'd noticed before the way Kristin hid behind a strong facade. This might be taking strength a little too far.

Lucas blocked her path, arms crossed over his chest. His next words might make her throw a few blows his way. She was a take-charge woman, always calling the shots when they trained together. She wasn't going to like him taking the lead. "You can't pretend nothing happened. You need to get checked out, make sure you aren't hurt, file a report. The police are on the way."

Sure enough, everything about her hardened, from her expression to her posture. "I'm fine. It was bound to happen sooner or later with me running alone out here. As for the police, shouldn't that have been my decision?" Kristin tried to push past him.

Lucas refused to budge. "You can take care of yourself. Got it. What about the next woman he targets? He left his mountain bike behind, and there are bound to be fingerprints. Don't you want the cops to find him before he tries again on a woman who can't shove him into a world of hurt?"

"He won't target—" Kristin turned her head and stared into the pine trees weaving gently in the wind. Finally, she sighed. "Fine. I'll wait in the parking lot." Without looking at either Lucas or Travis, she jogged away with only the slightest hitch to indicate she suffered any pain.

His instincts said she was hiding something. Lucas started to go after her but stopped. They might have formed a friendship, but it wasn't strong enough to force her to let him in. He'd wait until she put some distance between them then follow to make sure her attacker didn't swing around to try again.

Travis whistled low behind him. "We could've used that kind of grit in the platoon on this last deployment. She's got serious cool under fire."

Lucas kept his back to his buddy as he started a slow jog after Kristin, keeping her in sight. Sure, she was handling this well right now, but what would happen later?

And what was she not telling him?

TWO

Kristin's heart pounded, and it wasn't from exertion. That man had known who she was…had known who her brother, Kyle, was. This wasn't random, and until she figured out why, she wasn't telling the police or anyone else.

Kyle had spent his life in trouble. They'd spent the past decade apart, estranged after tragedy ripped their family into pieces, but he'd returned when he was stationed at Bragg, physically present even though his heart wasn't always in the game. He'd grown more distant after he deployed, though. Kristin had thought it was the stress of being overseas, but when he'd come home on R & R a few weeks before he died, something else was going on. He'd roamed the house at all hours, doing projects and generally not speaking, stoic like their father.

Their father.

Everything in her wanted to duck behind a tree and curl into a ball, maybe even lose what was left of the breakfast bar she'd crammed down before her run. No one had manhandled her in years, not since the night her father had pulled a knife on her mother, held the blade to Kristin's throat, then slashed his own wrists.

Cold sweat sheened her hot skin. Her attacker was no threat. She wouldn't let him be. Kristin had enough confidence in her physical condition to take on most men who didn't suspect her of being capable. But the memories? They threatened to bring on a full-fledged panic attack.

And she didn't panic. Ever.

Drawing in lungfuls of cool morning air, she tried to find comfort in the rhythm of her feet on the trail. *Left, right, left, right. Breathe.* It was over. If this guy returned, she could handle him.

And her father was dead. He couldn't hurt anyone anymore.

But he sure did have a way of reaching out of the grave to reignite her grief. Grief that had intensified when a sniper's bullet found her brother in Iraq.

Kristin scanned the trees, trying to find something, anything to focus on. The sky, the breeze, the chilled morning air…anything but what lay behind her, emotionally and physically.

Without turning around, Kristin knew Lucas and his friend would be close. From the brief couple of months they'd been running together, she had no doubt. Lucas was the kind who would protect even when he wasn't wanted.

She absolutely hated the comfort she felt. Knowing someone had her back unwound the tension. The smallest sliver inside wanted to stop and let them catch up, to not be alone.

That was scarier than anything else. In the face of the morning's events, seeing Lucas without time to prepare herself had sent a shudder through her insides. Every time they ran together, she'd had to school herself not to notice the way he made running seem effortless, the way his biceps peeked out from the sleeves of his T-shirt.

Man, she hated reacting to him. She usually didn't have a reaction to any guy at all. She'd always managed to stay detached, never engaging emotionally. She'd never had the dream of getting married, not after watching her parents claw and fight their way through their nasty, alcohol-fueled relationship. They'd stayed together out of some twisted kind of passion for one another. It was good in spurts. But when the passion flamed into anger, it was ugly for everybody within fist's reach.

Things in their family had grown uglier after her mother got sober and walked out when Kristin was sixteen, fighting to make life better for her children. But her father came at them again and again, was arrested and released over and over. Not even the law could save them. Her father had violated restraining orders until the day he ended everything.

That was all the proof Kristin needed. Being on fire for anybody was a bad thing. Emotions out of control led to lives out of control. She'd never wanted any part of feelings like those, had always avoided them.

But when it came to Lucas…he was a tough man to resist, and she'd tried her best. Those deep brown eyes had seen something inside her from the moment they'd crossed paths during a local half marathon and silently battled to the finish. Kristin had edged him out at the tape, but the conversation with Lucas after—and the realization he was responsible for the moving truck on

her street a few days earlier—had solidified a friendship played out in long runs through their neighborhood
when Kristin didn't run solo on the trails.

Runs that gradually grew longer as they started to
talk. Surface things at first, but lately she'd come dangerously close to feeding him information about her
past. He'd layered something soothing over her heart,
something that touched her insides every time she talked
to him, edging closer to things she'd never shared with
anyone else. They'd never done anything but train together, yet he made her feel like allowing someone else
inside her head was a good thing.

And everything had to stop. The morning's brutal reminder of her father's cruelty coupled with the mention
of her brother tore at her, chased her, drove her heart into
hiding. Her feet pounded harder, her breathing growing more ragged as emotions drove the pace until she
couldn't think anymore, couldn't even hear the outside
world over the thumping of her pulse in her ears. By the
time she hit the parking lot, her whole body hammered
in time with her heartbeat. She'd pushed too hard, but
the emotional and physical cleansing had been worth it.

Slowing to a fast walk, Kristin scanned the area,
glancing under her car in the distance to make sure no
one was beneath it. She shook it off, glancing at the
head of the trail.

Two military police vehicles stood blocking the entrance.

Kristin wanted to turn and run into the woods. Since
the night her mother had been murdered, she'd avoided
the police, even drove like a grandmother to wipe out
any possibility of a speeding ticket. The thought of an-

swering their pointed, dispassionate questions swirled bile in her stomach.

Besides, talking to them wouldn't change a thing. The justice system hadn't saved her mother.

She wouldn't talk to them. Lucas had made the call. He'd seen as much as she had, and he could do the talking.

Kristin whirled toward the woods, but only got an eyeful of Lucas and Travis coming off the trail.

Trapped. There was nowhere to go. Kristin marched for her small green SUV, wishing she were invisible, guilt biting at her heels. Lucas was right. Even though the man had mentioned Kyle, with her brother dead, they certainly couldn't ask him for his real motives. She ought to at least give a description to the police in case he tried to go after a woman who couldn't feed him his nose for breakfast.

Not that it would do any good to involve the law.

The debate raged as she stared at her SUV parked at the edge of the lot, but her feet slowed. Something wasn't right. There was no reflection from the driver's window. Surely she hadn't rolled it down.

Ignoring her rapidly tightening muscles, she jogged to her SUV, slowing as she neared. The window was shattered, glass littering the driver's seat. She punched the unlock code into the keypad and rounded the vehicle, ripping the passenger door open and scrambling across the seat. She jerked open the console to stare inside. Her wallet was where she always left it, but her keys were gone.

She dropped back, staring at the space where they'd been. That man had asked about her brother. Probably knew where she lived. And now he had her house keys. For the first time, the magnitude of the attack tackled her.

Feet pounded behind her. She didn't have to turn to know whom they belonged to. While she wanted to drop to the ground beside the car and curl into a fetal position, she swallowed her fears and stiffened her posture as she turned to meet Lucas Murphy head-on. "You can tell your cop friends someone stole my keys."

Behind him, Travis waved at the officers and detoured, jogging toward the military policemen at the head of the trail.

Lucas's eyebrow lifted. "Your keys were in your car?"

"It has a keypad lock. I lock them in when I run. It's better than dropping them in the woods somewhere." She slid out of the car and angled away from him, balling her fists and staring at the trees bordering the parking lot.

He was too close. His brown eyes too dark, his muscles beneath his T-shirt toned after his stint slogging through the desert overseas. The last thing she wanted to think about was how tempting it would be to let those arms hold her right now.

She ripped the headband from her hair and dragged her fingers through the tangle, probably standing it on end. She didn't care. This day had skidded into a ditch, and it wasn't even seven in the morning. Attacked on the trail. Stranded with only Lucas or the cops as her options for rescue. A strange man with her house keys.

Really. It couldn't get any worse.

THREE

"Dude, I think this might count as what normal people call 'a problem.'" Travis Heath's voice held the slightest thread of amusement as it drifted through the phone.

Lucas planted both feet onto the wide boards of his front porch and dug in his heels, but he didn't bother to answer. Travis would keep talking whether he responded or not.

"There are better things to do on a Thursday night. There's food. And friends. If any of the guys find out you're stalking some girl's house, your hero factor might fade a little."

Lucas didn't find any of this amusing. In fact, if he were the one on the other end of the phone, he'd probably forget the jokes and call the first sergeant to suggest a talking-to. Sitting on the porch to watch Kristin's house across the street ranked up there with one of the least rational things he'd ever done.

After the attack at Smith Lake, Lucas hadn't been able to get Kristin off his mind, although he'd tried. With the unit still getting into a routine after their deployment, the day was filled with mundane tasks, reestablishing a training schedule. He should have been focused on his job, but all his brain could do was scroll unbidden images of Kristin and replay conversations they'd had over the past couple of months. Their friendship might be young, but it ran deep, at least for him.

He couldn't speak for her, though. She'd bordered on telling him more personal things before, but she always checked herself, as if she were keeping a part of herself walled away. Maybe it was one-sided and she needed someone to train with, not a friend to tell her thoughts to.

Still, here he sat, anchored to a canvas chair, watching and waiting. Kristin had walked away today convinced the attack was a one-off, but Lucas couldn't help but believe there was more to it. He scrubbed at his cheek, wishing he could go in the house, watch a little TV, then hit the rack and sleep like a baby. But something—call it intuition or Jesus poking at him—said Kristin's run-in with a bad guy coupled with the theft of her keys was only the beginning. Being the victim of two random crimes at almost exactly the same time couldn't be coincidence.

He still couldn't shake the feeling she hadn't told him or the police everything. Something more had happened before Travis and he had come along. Lucas just couldn't figure out what.

"I lost you, didn't I?" Travis's voice drifted through the phone again. "No one can blame you for watching out for a friend, but don't cross the line from concerned friend to stalker."

Sergeant First Class Travis Heath knew Lucas better than anybody. They'd first met years ago in Ranger School, then been stationed together in their current assignment. As they worked as platoon sergeants, Travis in headquarters and Lucas in second platoon, they'd cemented a friendship, depending on each other in and out of the war zone. Travis always called it like he saw it, and he'd learned a lot from his own mistakes. If he felt like Lucas's porch surveillance was out-of-bounds, then it probably was, and he wouldn't hesitate to do what he could to keep Lucas from sinking into deeper trouble. "You think I'm crossing the line?"

"Only if you're attracted to her."

True, Kristin James was the most incredibly beautiful woman he'd ever laid eyes on, with short dark hair that waved around her face and blue eyes clear enough to see through to her thoughts...except this morning, when something about those eyes made it clear she was hiding part of her thoughts. She'd make any man do a double take. But knowing she was gorgeous didn't mean he felt anything more than friendship. "I'm not."

"Came back with that answer awfully fast, didn't you?" Once again, a smile laced Travis's accusation.

Really? Travis could think this was funny all he wanted, but none of this was laughable, especially since Travis's track record with women was pretty rough. Sure, Travis had changed over the past year, matured and dropped a whole host of bad habits, but he didn't need to be joking about relationships. His mistakes had sure made Lucas think twice about dating any woman when the military could swoop him up and send him off to anywhere in an instant.

Aside from any of that, some guy had targeted Kristin. He had her keys and likely knew where she lived. The part of him trained to defend couldn't let go. "I'm going to ask again. Do you think I'm crossing the line keeping an eye on her?"

"Are you kidding me?" Travis sobered, his earlier amusement gone. "I know your gut, Luke. It's better than a guided missile fixed on a target. You think something's going on, then you sit outside her house all night. If you're certain somebody's put a bull's-eye on her, then I'll take a shift later tonight so you can get some rest. But hey, don't be obvious. You're still the new guy in the neighborhood, and the last thing you need is a neighbor calling the cops on the creepy dude staring at the pretty lady's house. And definitely don't let Kristin see you. From what I saw today, she'll kick you into the next county herself." He exhaled loudly. "Man, do me a favor. If you're going to sit on the porch alone for hours, at least admit you feel something for her."

"I don't feel anything for Kristin James." He couldn't let himself. Lucas had spent years in a misguided search for meaning and relevance after his parents abandoned him on his aunt's doorstep. There was no counting how many people Lucas had hurt, how many women he'd used before a chaplain jerked him by the neck right after he graduated from basic training and called him on his self-destructive behavior, showed him what Jesus and grace and forgiveness could do in a man's life.

No, Lucas knew every man had limits, and he'd never cross a line with Kristin or any other woman again, at least not while the army called the shots.

"Lie to yourself all you'd like." Travis was far from finished. "I doubt you'd be standing watch if there wasn't a little bit of emotion involved." He paused. "Never mind. Scratch that. You would. It's how you're wired. Forgot who I was talking to."

"You finished yet?"

"No. I called for a reason. The commander called.

Criminal Investigation Command is sniffing around our guys."

"Why?"

"No idea. But keep a lookout. Something might be about to unleash."

Surely none of their men were in deep enough trouble to merit CID poking into the unit. They dealt with major crimes. Lucas let his eyes slip shut, trying to remember any local murders or assaults he'd seen on the news. Other than a specialist who'd come up hot on a drug test near the end of the deployment, nothing fit what CID might be searching for in their unit. They'd cut the guy loose last week and sent him packing. Yeah, Specialist Morrissey had been upset, but he wasn't the type of guy to do something to merit an investigation by CID. Then again, Lucas had been certain he wasn't the kind of guy to test positive, either.

"Here's the other thing. Maybe you need a break. You spent your post-deployment leave here, moving your stuff out of storage. Take a four-day. Get some actual time away. Shift that laser focus of yours to something besides your job."

Tempting, but Lucas wasn't ready to do nothing. His mind and his body were still on high alert from deployment. Sitting still sounded like a recipe for disaster until he totally unwound. "I'm doing a marathon next month. Can't disrupt training."

"Yeah, 'cause pounding pavement until your whole body threatens to fall out is relaxing. Or does training mean you get to spend more time with Kristin? You're prepping together for the same run, right?"

"Hanging up now. Had enough of your harassment. Go have fun with your buddies." Lucas shifted to press

End, knowing if the shoe was on the other foot, he'd be doing a whole lot more to provoke Travis.

"Hey, wait." Travis's urgency stopped Lucas from cutting the call. "If something goes down, you need to call the cops. Or at least call me. Don't go all hero and try to save the day without someone backing you up. If there's really somebody after Kristin James, there's a reason, and if they're willing to be as bold as they were today…"

Lucas's smile faded as he propped a foot on the porch rail. Travis was right. This was stupid. Monumentally, colossally stupid.

Yet he wasn't going anywhere. "I hear you." Lucas punched End without saying goodbye and stared at the small, square two-story brick house across the street. A second vehicle sat in the driveway, a Jeep Wrangler. Her friend Casey. Travis had met the other woman twice, but he couldn't remember a thing about her other than her dark green Jeep.

The house sat square in the small lot, the front door planted in the center of the structure, the windows on either side lit and casting deep shadows on the wide front porch. The little house sat across from his in the older Haymount neighborhood in Fayetteville, where the historic houses were gradually being overtaken and updated by those who saw value in their craftsmanship. He'd been in Kristin's house several times to work out in her basement gym when it was too rainy to get in a run, so he knew she'd put a lot of work into hers.

The memory made him grin. Kristin James might be a smashingly gorgeous woman, but she trained like a drill sergeant. He'd thought he was in shape and figured it would be easy to keep pace with her. Nope. She was a machine. No way he could forget the kind of bodily pain he'd felt after letting her unleash her personal trainer side during a weight-lifting session.

His smile faded. Kristin was small, but she was stronger than most men. She would be fine, and this stakeout was dumb. He was still in combat mode, seeing monsters in the shadows. Kristin was safe, and he needed to wrap this up, for his own sanity.

He pushed himself out of the chair, but a flash from the corner of the house near her car stopped him.

Lucas squinted against the darkness, wishing he could bolt across the street and demand some identification from the shadowy figure skirting between the vehicles in her driveway. But if it was a neighbor searching for a lost cat, he'd have a whole lot of questions coming and no good way to answer any of them.

The flashlight bobbed under a window then to the far corner of the house, where the gate to the backyard stood in the huge wooden privacy fence. The flashlight paused, and then the gate slipped open and the silhouette of a man vanished.

The floor joists creaked as Kristin paced the small kitchen on the side of the house, listening to the coffee-maker whir as it heated water. The muscles in her legs ached their protest. After her run today, she'd been too keyed up to stretch, and the tension of the morning had settled in to stay. She'd met with clients all day, coaching them through their workouts, then come home and pounded the punching bag in the basement until her arm muscles quivered. Nothing had helped the stress.

Maybe she ought to tackle painting the guest bathroom. She'd been putting it off, but painting would give her something to do tonight while she wasn't sleeping. Renovations on the old house in the fast-rising Haymount neighborhood were coming slowly, but the basement and the first floor were done. Kristin paced the length of the kitchen again, staring at the original hardwood, polished to a satiny sheen. Tearing out layers of linoleum had been backbreaking but worth it.

"You could make a three-toed sloth so nervous it would run for the next county." Kristin's best friend, Casey Jordan, stood in the arched kitchen doorway, holding a dog-eared and worn book of sudoku puzzles, her shoulder-length blond hair pulled away from her face with a butterfly clip.

"Yeah, well, I think I need to lace my shoes and run a few miles." Maybe she could talk Lucas into going with her. Except that would be the dumbest thing ever. With her emotions twisted, the last thing she needed to do was give him free rein with her feelings.

"Running is what got you into trouble in the first place."

"Running is my therapy, like you and your crazy number puzzles." Casey was talking about this morning's trail run, but she was right on so many other levels. Running with Lucas had started something Kristin probably needed to stop. Even though she really didn't want to. Kristin bounced on her toes, nervous energy pushing against her skin, searching for a way out. She pressed the brew button on the coffee machine then turned to her best friend. "You didn't have to come over."

"Sure, I did. And number puzzles make me happy."

"You're addicted."

"Nice try swinging this to me. After what happened

to you this morning, I couldn't leave you here lying awake while you listen for things that go bump in the night." Casey held up a hand to stop Kristin's argument before it could form. "I know exactly what you're going to say. You don't scare easily, but knowing some guy out there has your house key can't be comforting, especially after—"

"Can we change the subject?" Kristin didn't want to think about it, but the twinge in her shoulder blade where she'd smashed into the tree kept her from forgetting.

The keys bugged her. Taking her keys and leaving everything else behind felt personal. She'd had the fob for her house alarm deactivated and made sure to set the alarm when she left to work, but that hadn't brought her a whole lot of comfort. It was doubtful the police would get there fast enough, even with a monitored system. When the system went off last week, it took forever to trigger a phone call to her cell. Her mother's home alarm hadn't been a fast enough response the night her dad had lost it. The deed was done before the alarm company could respond.

"The locksmith came this afternoon and rekeyed the locks." Still, if somebody wanted in bad enough, a lack of keys wouldn't stop them. The guy was determined. He had known who she was, had mentioned Kyle by name. There was more to this than the surface told, but she couldn't begin to guess what.

Not that she'd admit any of her fears to Casey. Still, it would be a relief to know Casey was bunked in the downstairs guest room. Kristin could take care of herself, but having an army staff sergeant to back her up wouldn't be a bad thing.

She pulled the huge mug of coffee from the machine and handed it over, then grabbed a bottle of water from the fridge and an orange from the bowl on the table, following the other woman into the living room.

Sinking onto the sofa, Kristin started to set her water on the coffee table, but a soft sound from the side of the house kept the bottle hovering. Probably the wind. Or one of the cats that roamed the neighborhood after dark. She set the water on the table harder than she should have. Stupid day making her paranoid.

Casey curled her feet under her in a blue-and-white-striped wing-back chair and laid her book on the end table. "So…let's talk about who played your knight in shining armor today."

Kristin's stomach sank. She should have known this was coming. Casey knew Kristin's stance on dating, but the woman relished a good love story.

Well, there sure wasn't one here. Kristin dug her thumb into the orange, releasing a soft citrusy spray, then pulled back the peel. "Nothing to talk about. Lucas and his buddy came around the corner. He chased the guy and called the cops while Travis acted like I was some weak female who needed his help."

"Sounds like they played cleanup after you took care of the problem yourself."

Kristin smiled and tipped the water bottle, taking a long drink. She'd defended herself quite nicely, if she did say so herself. If there was anything good about this day, it was the way she'd proved her strength, even if part of it was to herself.

"Too bad you can't use the incident in your advertising and branch out into self-defense classes."

No. The thought was a little tempting, but Kristin

would never glorify an attacker by using his twisted behavior to sell her own skills. "I've got my hands full with personal training clients and hanging out with you." Not to mention, the idea of having to defend herself if the guy returned wanting to talk about Kyle had her stomach knotted like a rope hammock.

"Hanging out with me. Whatever." Casey waved a hand in the air, but Kristin could see it on her face. Under the tough-girl mask she always wore, Casey never could quite believe she was good enough, had said more than once she couldn't understand why someone like Kristin would ever want to be her friend. Every time she said it, Kristin wanted to hug Casey and reassure her of her own awesomeness.

Before Kristin could say anything, Casey shifted in her seat. "What are you not telling me? Is there something more between you and this Lucas guy?"

"Absolutely nothing."

"Kris…"

"You know what I can't get out of my head?" If Kristin could possibly change the direction of this conversation, she was going to do it.

"What's that?"

"The guy who came at me today…he had this tattoo." She shuddered. Couldn't help it. The thing was gruesome. "This snake on his leg. Wrapped all the way around his calf, dripping blood… I've never seen anything like it."

"You told the cops? That's a seriously strong identifier."

"I did."

"And you're not getting me off track. That's not the

thing you're hiding." Casey arched an eyebrow in that knowing way she had. "I want to hear about—"

"The guy who came at me on the trail mentioned Kyle. By name." She winced, hating she'd confessed that much, but even though it invited more scrutiny, it was the one way to shake Casey off the Lucas thing.

"What?" Casey leaned forward and set her mug on the table hard, coffee sloshing onto the dark wood. She swiped the spot with her fingertips. "You were targeted? Because of your brother?"

"Looks like."

"Why? What did the punk do to—"

"Kyle's dead, Case. I get it—you never trusted him. But he was still my brother."

"Who ditched you for years and only showed his face because he needed a place to crash." The hardness in Casey's expression faded, and she sat back, pulling at the hem of her purple Carolina Beach sweatshirt. "I'm sorry. He's gone, and I should watch my mouth."

"He was trying." Kristin hated the weakness in her voice. Her brother had been the only family she'd had left. When they were small, he'd always played protector, even though he was a year younger. They'd been close, each other's best friend and closest companion. He'd defended Kristin at every chance, though he never witnessed their father's brutality. Kristin had protected him from the truth as much as possible, and Kyle had idolized the man. He'd run away shortly after their parents' deaths, refusing to believe their father had done something so heinous. While Kristin had spent the remainder of her high school years with their grandmother, taking on her mother's maiden name after refusing to be known by her father's anymore, Kyle had wandered, staying with distant relatives and friends, generally getting into trouble before deciding to make the army his life. Those last few months before he deployed, when he'd been stationed at Bragg, had reunited the siblings, however briefly.

While Kyle was still a bit of a loose cannon, he'd matured. Other than being basically silent about anything personal, he'd seemed normal…for this new, more distant version of Kyle. He'd even helped her finish the basement before he deployed, using some of the skills he'd learned earning money in high school to put in drywall and paint. Other than his utter failure at communicating, those few weeks had been good.

When he'd been killed, he'd left Kristin his life insurance and the '68 Camaro he'd been restoring in her detached garage. While she'd often sat in the front seat of the car and toyed with the idea of turning the key, she hadn't had the heart to drive it. It was his baby, the one thing he'd been enthusiastic about.

"Listen, Kris…"

Kristin shook her head. "Don't worry about it. I admit he could be—" A crash from the backyard brought her to her feet, and she was halfway to the door before she realized she was plunging headfirst into danger…like her mother had on the night she died.

FOUR

With Casey close behind, Kristin flipped on the flood-lights and shoved through the door onto the low deck, the evening chill a stark contrast to the warmth inside.

Two men were locked in battle at the corner of the house, one besting the other.

A very familiar one besting the other. This couldn't be happening. None of this could be happening. Heart hammering, Kristin jumped the steps into the yard. "What is going on here?"

The masked man Lucas had pinned by the chest to the privacy fence took advantage of the momentary distraction. Twisting sideways and throwing his elbow up, he caught Lucas in the chin, relaxing the hold enough to duck and run for the front yard.

Casey bolted into the house. "I'm on it."

"Casey, don't." Too late. She'd already disappeared. That drive to be helpful was going to be her downfall someday.

As Kristin gathered herself and joined the pursuit, Lucas ran for the gate, pounding his palm against the rough wood as tires screeched on a side street two houses away. When he turned toward Kristin, the shad-

ows in the side yard cast a fierce mask over his countenance, deepening his eyes and highlighting the strong
set of his jaw.

The sight of him almost drove Kristin back, but the
fear zinging through her had nothing to do with the man
and everything to do with her reaction. Lucas Murphy
was gradually inching a hold around her heart.

And he'd been knee-deep in two questionable situ-
ations on the same day. With her emotions tangled and
the other threat gone, everything focused on Lucas,
Kristin's brain spinning too fast to acknowledge the
enormity of what was truly happening.

Kristin squared her shoulders, half to take authority
and half to warn her galloping heartbeat that now was
not the time. Lucas couldn't continue to jump in to save
her. She didn't need it. Didn't want it. Couldn't he grasp
she could handle this? "What are you doing here?"

He ought to look like a sheepish little boy caught
stealing from his grandmother's cookie jar. Instead, he
tipped his chin in defiance and strode closer with an air
of belonging, his shoulders squared like he was ready to
do battle all over again, this time with her. "I'm making short work of the guy who tried to break into your
house."

She wasn't sure what spiked her blood pressure more—
someone trying to violate her life for the third time in one
day, or Lucas playing witness and would-be protector.
They were supposed to be casual acquaintances, borderline friends, not some damsel in distress and her knight
in shining armor. "I can take care of myself. Casey and I
were both here, and I'm—"

"Not being very vigilant."

Her body stiffened so fast it brought on an instant

tension headache. The fear and anger at the people trying to infiltrate her life focused like a laser on the closest target in range. "I'm starting to wonder if you are absolutely nothing short of bad news."

"What's that supposed to mean?"

"It means my life was perfectly, absolutely sane until you showed up in it. We've been training together for two months, and before then, no one ever tried to attack me or break into my house. You want to talk about threats? You know my routine almost better than I do. You know the trails I run on the days you and I don't run together. So tell me, Lucas…this morning? Right now? Right place, right time? Or is this some half-cocked effort to—"

His eyes widened, and if it were possible, they'd have shot fire. "You think I have something to do with this?"

"If the shoe fits."

Casey jogged out the door onto the deck, deflecting some of the tension. "Lost the guy. Got a partial plate." She planted her hands on her hips, watching the tennis match between Kristin and Lucas. "Want me to call the—"

"No." Kristin turned away from the man who somehow managed to nudge guilt around the edges of her emotions. They might not be best buds, but she knew him well enough to know he wasn't the kind of creep she was implying he was. Sure, common sense said she ought to suspect him, but her mind knew better.

It would be impossible to face him with her accusation hanging in the air. She took two steps onto the deck toward Casey. "No cops. They won't do anything. They can't." She kept right on talking, trying to stop the argument she knew Casey was putting together. "My house. My rules. No cops." She couldn't get a restraining order against a man whose name she didn't even know, and it hadn't helped her mother to have one anyway. Nor could she expect an officer to sit outside her house in case somebody tried to break in again. She was trained. She was strong. She was fearless. It was a trifecta she trusted.

"You're being foolish, Kris." Lucas's voice came from behind her, closer this time.

Her skin chilled at the nickname in his deep voice, too much like the way her father used to say it. "It's Kristin." She turned to offer a half apology, to tell him he might not be a stalker but he definitely wasn't her hero. The words never formed.

He'd edged closer, a few feet away at the bottom of the steps, fully illuminated by the floodlights. Blood ran from the corner of his right eye, and a red spot marred his chin where a bruise would likely form tomorrow. He'd put himself in the line of fire…for her.

She couldn't yell at him then send him packing after he'd put himself between her and danger twice. Kristin hated herself for being soft. For noting the way his eyes had gold flecks in them, the way he stood like he had all the authority in the world, not with a challenge, but in a way that made her feel protected.

It also made the guilt from accusing him twist even harder. That couldn't be left out there, pulling tight between them. Kristin blew her bangs out of her face and stared at a spot on the fence over Lucas's shoulder. "Listen. I'm sorry. What I said earlier… I know you're not—"

"I know." Lucas didn't even let her finish, probably understanding the way the unfamiliar apology stuck in her throat. He knew her too well, was probably nicer than she deserved.

She sliced the air with her hands, helpless to hold on to her anger and the distance she desperately needed to put between herself and Lucas.

Tomorrow. Tomorrow she could pull away, call a halt to this building friendship before the feelings grew until they scorched her into ashes. Before she turned into her mother and lost everything to a complete, emotion-fueled fall from grace. "Get inside before you bleed all over your shirt."

Near the door, Casey cleared her throat. "I'm going to go…" She jerked her thumb over her shoulder, flustered by something Kristin couldn't even begin to imagine. "Inside. Somewhere. And be…inside." She slipped through the door and disappeared into the house, probably calling the police against Kristin's wishes.

Kristin sighed and looked down at Lucas, surrendering the fight. "I guess you're going to tell me I should see the other guy, huh?"

"It's a wonder he was able to walk away," Lucas said as he quirked a half smile, avoiding movement on the injured side of his face but lighting the eyes Kristin was trying hard not to notice. "You know, I had him till someone distracted me."

Kristin rolled her eyes and ignored the flicker of fear threatening to flame up. Regardless of anything else, someone had been in her backyard. But she was fearless, right? She flicked her hand toward the door. "Get in the house. And stop talking before I decide to bruise your other cheek." She turned and headed for the door, her heart hammering.

Letting Lucas Murphy in might be even more dangerous than any stranger trying to invade her home.

Lucas followed Kristin into the kitchen, clenching and unclenching his fists. He'd seen the fear flash on her face, understood better than anyone how it could toy with thoughts and make them completely whacked. There had been times when he'd felt that edge himself overseas, maybe even bordered a little on paranoid, particularly after one of their soldiers was killed by a sniper while on guard duty. But being on the receiving end of Kristin's suspicion had been worse than any blow his opponent had thrown earlier.

It still stung, even after her apology, something that had to be hard for her "no surrender" self. But as soon as she'd shown that small crack, she'd rebuilt the wall, acting once again like she could control the whole world.

She walked ahead of him, not waiting to see if he followed, her posture arrow straight. Her attitude made Lucas want to grab her shoulder and stop her, to turn her around and force a confrontation, to ask if she really had so little trust in him.

Except, really, what right did he have to ask? Whether it hurt or not, in her position he might have fired off some of the same questions. He surveyed the kitchen, searching for something, anything to focus on long enough to stem the chaos roiling in his head.

The control-freak side of Kristin came out in her home. The polished hardwood was spotless. The dark wood cabinets harbored no dust. No photos, no knickknacks, nothing broke the smooth surface of the marble counter. Everything had a place. From what little she'd told him on their morning runs, he knew her childhood had been chaotic, and the early chaos came out in her need for strict order as an adult.

She'd have made an amazing military officer.

He inhaled deeply, centering himself in where he was. The place had a scent of its own. Not like some houses, all cinnamon and spice. More like outdoors and oranges. Probably from the bowl she kept on the table. Every time they worked out together, she'd dig into an orange after, always offering him one before she slipped into one of the chairs at the kitchen table to peel the fruit and savor it like other women savored chocolate.

He'd never been a fan of oranges before, but lately he'd acquired the taste.

Lucas shut the door behind him, wanting to sink into one of the chairs at the small breakfast table where they'd shared a handful of meals after workouts. The woman might be tough as nails, but she could cook like nobody's business. Probably because her inner control freak didn't trust anyone else to touch her food.

Kristin passed the small table in the breakfast nook and pulled one of the black wood chairs out. "Have a seat and we'll see if we can make you look less like you went a few rounds in the Ultimate Fighting Championship." Without looking back to make sure he obeyed, she charged through the arched doorway to the dining room.

Lucas could hear her footsteps on the stairs, either to find a first-aid kit or to break the phone he was pretty certain Casey was using to call the police.

Dropping into the chair, Lucas stared at the door. Whoever had come after Kristin at Smith Lake today had likely been watching her, had known which car was hers and had taken the opportunity to steal her keys and her address, probably off her registration. The scum had liked what he'd seen and had decided to come after it in spite of the fact Casey's Jeep in the driveway proved Kristin wasn't home alone.

The thought of someone hurting Kristin made him run hot with anger and cold with fear. Even though Travis tried to imply differently, Kristin was a friend, and Lucas would do what he had to do to protect her.

He pressed a finger gingerly to his cheek. Even if he had to do battle with shadowy men in her backyard.

Kristin came into the room and dropped a first-aid kit onto the table, then laid a damp washcloth beside it. She pulled out the chair across from him and sat, tipping her head toward the items in front of him. "You look a mess. The cut by your eye you can probably camouflage a little bit. You're lucky the guy didn't leave a worse mark on your chin. Not sure how your chain of command would like you looking like the loser in a fistfight."

His chain of command was a worry for tomorrow. "Loser? I'm pretty sure I look like the winner." He grabbed the washcloth and weighed it in his hand, unable to help himself. "Are you sure you don't want to do this for me? Like in the movies? Help the poor hero who was injured when he managed to—"

"Don't push it." She sat back in the chair and crossed her arms over her chest, the words harsh but her blue eyes not backing up the sass.

Those eyes. He dropped his to the first-aid kit. It would be way too easy to stare into hers when he knew better. The way she leveled those crystal blues on him dragged a longing into his chest. One he hadn't felt in a long time… One that made him sit straight in the chair and fight for air. He squeezed the damp cloth until water dripped onto his thigh and seeped through his blue jeans. *Get over yourself, Murphy.* No sense in dragging her into a life-style that would only tear them apart when he left.

He stared at the dark spots the water had left on his thigh, wresting control of his rogue thoughts before he pressed the cloth to the corner of his eye. "Casey called the police?"

"You read people well. She did. But really, what can they do? They're going to come here, ask some ques-tions. They'll want to talk to you, I'm sure, but later? They'll put out an extra patrol and an officer will come by once an hour or something. It's not enough to put my faith in. They're too understaffed to do more, and patrols leave too many gaps in the meantime for some-one to try again." Her words were matter-of-fact, but her fingers tightened around her biceps. She might not want to admit it, but the day's events weighed on her. The strain showed in the straight lines of her posture and the sharp angles of her words.

"The guy has your keys."

"The locksmith changed my locks today, and I had the fob for the alarm disabled. They won't do him any good." She leaned forward and propped her elbows on the table. "Lucas, really. How did you manage to be here tonight right when you needed to be? And don't try to tell me you happened to walk by your front window."

Lucas checked the cloth and reached for the first-aid kit, digging for anything that might stop the sting near his eye. He really didn't want to explain what he was doing here tonight, but he'd never lied to her before and he wasn't about to start now. "I was worried. I knew the guy had your keys, so…" Saying *I was sitting across the street watching your house* sounded a whole lot better in theory than it was ever going to sound in person. In person, it sounded like he'd bounced his marbles halfway to Smoke Bomb Hill on the east side of Fort Bragg.

"So you thought you'd pull guard duty." She sighed and stared at the closed plantation blinds over the side window, shaking her head. "You're crazy."

"Don't I know it."

She chuckled. "Really. I think I proved this morning I can take care of myself. And Casey's here." She aimed a finger at the door, her expression softening. "Go home. I know you have to work in the morning, and you can't lose sleep watching over me forever."

Everything she said made logical sense, but he couldn't make himself agree with her. All he could see was that monster of a man slamming her into a tree this morning. The replay always stopped right before Kristin sent the guy running with his tail between his legs and spun a whole new horrible version of what might have been. "How bad is your back hurting right now?"

Her head drew back like she was dodging a blow. She eyed him for a minute before she took an orange from the bowl and rolled it between her palms. "Not as bad as you'd think. A little sore in the shoulder blade, but not enough to slow me down." She dropped the orange and rolled it across the table toward him. "Thanks for asking."

"No problem." Lucas rolled the orange to her. "And I'm sleeping on your couch tonight."

They shared an elementary school–style stare-down before she turned away and stretched across the table, dragging the red canvas first-aid kit toward her. "I'll make a deal with you." She dug through until she found a butterfly bandage, then slid it toward him. "For your eye."

"What's the deal?" He didn't reach for the bandage. If he finished doctoring himself, she'd kick him out of the house.

"I've got an alarm. A loud one. If something goes bump in the night, you won't be able to sleep through it." The doorbell echoed through the room, and Kristin pushed away from the table, grimacing. "Final offer, superhero. Take it or I'll tell the cops you're part of the problem then send you and Casey both home."

Lucas hesitated, then reached for the bandage on the table with a nod. Fine. He'd leave.

But she couldn't keep him from sitting on his own front porch.

FIVE

Kristin shifted her small SUV into Park and killed the engine, staring at the brick building in front of her. She twisted her hands on the steering wheel, watching soldiers filter out of the building for lunch, hoping Lucas wasn't one of them. She knew this was his area, knew her brother had been in the same battalion. Although the chances the two of them had crossed paths were slim, the last thing she wanted to do was run into him.

The conversation in her kitchen last night had been awkward at best, uncomfortable at worst. He'd sat across from her, bleeding, while her fingers itched to help him. The problem was, something under her skin was reacting to his presence, to his macho hero actions in her yard. Touching him, even to bandage his eye, would have gone exactly like he'd joked—like a movie. It would have ended with her looking way too deeply into his brown eyes and wanting nothing more than to kiss him. It had been a relief when he went home. Even more of a relief when she'd peeked out the window somewhere in the middle of her long, sleepless night and seen his shadow move on his front porch.

She'd never had a panic attack, not even the night her

mother died, but the thought of feeling this strongly for Lucas Murphy bordered on the most terrifying thing she'd faced since. It would lead to trouble. Lots of trouble.

So the last thing she wanted was to run into him on this fool's errand for one of her brother's buddies. She surveyed the soldiers again, looking for one who seemed familiar.

A tall, thin soldier broke away from the pack and headed her way with a determined stride. Specialist Brandon Lacey had come to her house a few times to work on Kyle's beloved Camaro with him, and he'd written twice after Kyle died, working out his own grief. Kristin's overall impression had always been of a tall, lanky kid who was still trying to get comfortable in his adult skin. He walked with more confidence now, post deployment, but he still gave off a slightly awkward air.

She reached for the shoebox-size package on the passenger seat and slipped out of the SUV, her bruised shoulder blade protesting the lateral movement, and stayed close to the vehicle so she could get away before Lucas somehow appeared and got the wrong idea. The last thing she needed was him thinking she'd decided to stalk him, even though he'd done a fair job of making himself right at home in her immediate vicinity.

At the sight of her, Specialist Lacey broke into a grin and jogged closer. "Kristin, I'd remember you anywhere. Hard to forget those crazy blue eyes."

Yeah, yeah. Sure. She'd like just once to meet someone and have them not talk about her eyes. "It's me." She shoved the package toward Lacey. "He sent this to me right before…" It was still too hard to say. *He died.* The last of her blood family, gone.

She shook it off, wanting to get this over as fast as possible, both to keep Lucas from spotting her and to keep Brandon Lacey from staring at her like he'd never seen a woman before. "Anyway, he said it was some stuff you didn't want sent to your parents' address and he'd…" *Take care of it when he came home.*

Brandon didn't seem to notice Kristin's discomfort, just grinned wider as he took the package and tucked it under his arm. "Bought my mom a few things from a market over there. Kyle being in the mail room made it easier for him to get things out than for me to pack them in my ruck. She's coming here to visit soon, so it'll be good to have it. Thanks." His grin faded, and his face fell under his beret. "Like I said when I wrote you, I'm sorry about Kyle. He was a good friend. Liked to skate the line a little, but he had a buddy's back when he needed it."

Kristin pressed her lips together and nodded, flicking a glance over the kid's shoulder as he talked. The flow of soldiers heading out to lunch had slowed to a trickle. Maybe Lucas was working through. Or maybe he'd left. Either way, she wanted out before he appeared or Lacey drifted into some sentimental place and started telling stories she wasn't ready to hear. Maybe someday…

"Thanks." She held up her watch, making a show of checking the time. "I've got a training client in an hour, so I need to get going. If I find anything else I think you might want when I get Kyle's things, I'll let you know."

Brandon started to leave then stopped, head tilting. "You don't have his stuff yet? They didn't send it when he died?"

"No. I didn't expect to see anything until you guys all returned." Truth was, she was in no hurry. Digging through her brother's life felt wrong, especially given their brokenness.

"Hmm." He bobbed a nod, then looked at a tight-knit group of soldiers standing about a hundred feet away, watching with interest.

No telling what they thought her relationship with this kid was. He was a good five years younger than her. Probably more. Well, they could think whatever they wanted, but thinking wouldn't make it true.

"Well, if I can speed anything up for you, I will, but you know, my rank's not high enough to order anyone around. Have a good one. And thanks for dropping this off." He tossed a wave and jogged to his buddies, who were uncharacteristically silent, from what she knew of young soldiers.

"What are you doing here?" The voice at her elbow made her jump.

Kristin grabbed the door to steady herself, her heart jerking into her throat then dropping into her shoes. Lucas. She hadn't made it out fast enough.

"You look like you're not so happy to see me." His eyebrow lifted in question, though he seemed amused. "Did you need me for something?"

Her face was probably twisted into a scowl, not welcoming and definitely unfriendly. He stood so close the warmth of him telegraphed to her, firing whatever she'd felt last night all over again. "No, I'm not here stalking you." Her voice cracked, so she swallowed the jagged edges of attraction and slid into the SUV, desperate for distance. "I had to bring my brother's friend something."

She reached for the door, but he held tight above the window. "I didn't know you had a brother."

Kristin stared out the windshield, refusing to look at him. She'd chosen to keep Kyle's association with Lucas to herself because their complicated relationship opened doors to questions that led to too many things she didn't want to talk about. "It's not something I'm ready to talk about." Like the fact she hated to be treated like a weak female. And she hated the way she noticed how he smelled like soap and outdoors.

"But you have a brother."

"It didn't seem relevant."

He tipped his head and leaned closer, curiosity arching his eyebrow. "He's in my battalion? Who is he? Maybe—"

"He's dead, Lucas." She stared at the center of the steering wheel, tears she usually didn't shed kicking at her eyes. "A sniper killed him."

Lucas's hand fell from the door. "When?" Something in his voice was tight, like he'd wound the words around one of those old-fashioned tops and was waiting to pull the string.

"About four months ago."

"Kyle Coleman?"

She winced, her brother's name in Lucas's mouth like crossing two universes. It was part of the reason she'd never mentioned Kyle to him in the first place. The two pieces of her life didn't mesh. "Yes." She reached for the door and grabbed the handle. "I have to go. I'll—I'll see you later." This was too much. Her brother. Lucas. Feeling.

He backed away and let her slam the door with a little too much force, even though he acted like he had so much more to say.

Kristin wrenched the key in the ignition and jammed

her SUV into Reverse. Lucas thought some crazy guy with her house key was a problem. As far as she was concerned, the biggest danger in her life right now was letting her emotions get tangled with Lucas Murphy.

Lucas stared at his computer screen, reading the Record of Emergency Data for Specialist Kyle Coleman, unable to deny what he saw. Coleman's sister listed as next of kin.

Kristin James.

Her name tensed every muscle in his body. Lucas wanted to pace the room, but that would draw the attention of his first sergeant and a CID agent who stood talking in the hall. Three agents had arrived after the soldiers left for lunch. With the events of the past couple of days, he'd forgotten Travis's warning. Seemed like they were about to find out which of their guys was in trouble...and why.

Right now, though, he had to deal with his own problems. Now he had double the reason to downshift this attraction to Kristin. He wouldn't date the sister of one of his soldiers, even one who was gone. It crossed too many lines, made things too volatile.

Under cover of his desk, Lucas balled his fists and pressed them into his knees, thankful the men outside were engrossed in their conversation. He didn't want to think about any of this, let alone talk about it with Travis or CID, not when he couldn't fully explain her silence and his feelings to himself.

Specialist Kyle Coleman had barely made the cut as a soldier. He'd made no secret of the fact he'd joined the army for the sign-up bonus, and he was broke more often than not. He'd found every way to skirt the rules and to flout authority. The kid had been a slacker, mouthy and disrespectful. So much so that he'd been busted down a rank and had to work his way to specialist all over again, a slow climb due to continued borderline behavior. Coleman had spent about a month in Lucas's platoon before getting sent to the S1 shop, working in the mail room. He'd been nothing but trouble…

Until a bullet found him while he was on guard duty.

Specialist Coleman had done a lot of things, but nothing deserved death, especially not at the hands of a cowardly terrorist.

Lucas scrubbed the back of his neck. Why hadn't Kristin told him? Seemed easy enough. "You're in the First of the 504th? So was my brother. Small world, huh?" Keeping quiet made no sense, unless she hadn't realized they were in the same unit. The possibility was remote. The information hadn't surprised her, and if she'd sent her brother mail, she'd have written the unit designation right on the envelope. It made no—

Three taps on the metal door frame jerked him to attention. Travis and the CID agent stood there, watching him.

Travis stepped into the room first. "You busy?" The silent question he fired Lucas's way was stronger. *What's wrong?*

Nothing he wanted to discuss. He stood and turned to the stranger at Travis's side. "Sergeant First Class Lucas Murphy."

"Major Randall Draper." The agent dipped a chin. "Murphy. You get a lot of flak for that name?"

Too much. "Private Murphy's Law" was a well-known comic strip about army life, and Murphy's Laws of Combat had been around forever. While both were spot-on,

Lucas had grown tired of the comparison. He faked a smile and hoped it looked real. "More than I ever wanted."

The major grinned, then dropped the humor just as fast. "It's time we filled you in on what's going on in the battalion."

Lucas aimed a finger at a nearby chair and sank into his own. Right now was the time to shut the lid on his personal life box and open the professional one. Whatever was happening, the look on the major's face said it was serious. Lucas braced himself.

Draper wasted no time, speaking before he'd even settled into the chair. He swept a hand over his dark hair. "Over the years, you've probably heard how we've had some issues with missing antiquities in Iraq. Civilians, contractors, even a few of our guys grabbing art and small artifacts as souvenirs or to sell off. We started checking equipment coming back, caught a few guys bringing things in rucksacks and Conex containers, but it's been mostly small stuff, souvenirs, innocent pilfering. Illegal, yes, but nothing on the level of a smuggling ring."

"Something escalated?" Lucas glanced at Travis, who sat stone-faced, probably hearing this for the second time. "What's this got to do with our guys?"

"Some of the items have shown up on the black market, been advertised on the dark web. We picked up chatter from your area of operations and traced it to some computers on your forward operating base. Some pretty valuable items were brokered when you guys were deployed, and some had multiple buyers for the same item. There's a lot we're still deciphering, but someone in this battalion was the deliveryman. The items weren't large—some vases, a few sculptures—but they have value and are highly collectible. They were never delivered, and we believe they're in the States somewhere. We're interested in the specialist who was killed on guard duty near the end of the tour."

Lucas schooled his reaction, calling on every trick he'd ever devised to keep his face impassive. Kristin's brother. Kristin…whom he had seen handing off a package to another soldier.

His gut clenched like he'd run a twenty-miler without hydrating first. No. *Please, God. Please let this all be a huge misunderstanding.*

Draper nodded, unaware of the war going on inside Lucas, but it was Travis who spoke. "They're not prepared to say Coleman was involved, but his death was unusual."

"How?" Lucas's voice was tight, a rubber band ready to snap.

Travis noticed, but he only arched an eyebrow.

Draper stared at something outside the window. "Blood spatter at the scene indicated he was shot by someone inside the forward operating base."

"And we're just hearing this now?" There was no reason to hide the anger. CID knew the shooting was from inside their FOB and no one had told them there might be danger?

"Active investigation."

Lucas slammed his palm on the desk, but a quick cough from Travis stopped him from unleashing on a ranking officer. Major Draper was merely the messenger. There was no reason to invite trouble by letting his anger loose now. His mind raced. Kristin's brother might have been murdered by one of their own, and she might be involved. This had to be a nightmare. "You think Coleman was involved and it got him killed?"

"It's a distinct possibility." Major Draper hardly batted an eye. "Since he was in your platoon for a short time before he went to Sergeant Heath's platoon, we wanted anything you might remember. Anything would be helpful."

"I can't think of much," Travis said. "Coleman wasn't fun, but nothing said he was doing anything like you're suggesting."

Lucas wrestled his anger into place and recounted what he could remember, with Travis furnishing additional details. "Honestly? Other than being a slacker, nothing stood out about Coleman." He kept his eyes off the computer screen. Nothing stood out until now.

Travis sat forward, resting a hand on the edge of Lucas's desk. "What are you not saying?" He'd always been able to read Lucas, ever since the first day they'd met at Ranger School. Being stationed together at Bragg had contributed to a company that worked well because the platoon sergeants knew each other, respected each other and could tell what the other was thinking.

Lucas addressed Travis. "It's Kristin."

"What about her?"

"Kristin James?" Major Draper sat straighter. "You know her?"

"She's my neighbor." Lucas turned the computer screen toward Travis. "She's Coleman's sister."

"You didn't know?" Travis turned from the screen to Lucas.

"Didn't even know she had a brother until today." His gut dropped clear to his boots. He didn't want to say what he had to say next. "She was here earlier."

Draper's eyes narrowed. "To see you?"

Lucas ground his teeth together, unsure what to say.

If Kristin was innocent, she didn't need Lucas casting suspicion on her. If she was guilty...

No. He was certain she was innocent. She had to be.

"Who was she here to see, Sergeant?"

"Specialist Lacey." Lucas braced, waiting to see if Draper reacted to the name.

Draper didn't flinch as he keyed something into his phone. "Know why?" He didn't look up, just kept his thumb poised and ready to type.

Lucas stood, trying to get on level ground with the other man. What he was about to say looked bad. Really bad. "Dropping off a package." He held out a hand as the other men's heads lifted. "Something her brother mailed to her for Lacey. I'm certain—"

"Certain what, Sergeant?" Draper lowered his phone. "Certain she can't be a criminal because you're friends?"

"With all due respect, I think questioning Sergeant Murphy is pointless, sir." Travis stood and stared down at the major, coming awfully close to being insubordinate. "He's a good judge of character. They know each other well."

Lucas tried not to flinch. That made everything sound so...trashy.

Draper was clearly thinking the same thing. He stood and slipped his phone into his pocket, pinning Lucas with a hard glare. "Sergeant, I'm pretty sure I don't have to tell you to keep your mouth shut around this girl. In fact, I'm pretty sure we don't need to talk about having contact with her at all."

Lucas stiffened. Surely the major wasn't about to tell him to cut ties. He couldn't. What if CID was right and her brother was involved in something out-of-bounds? "Sir, Kristin James was attacked yesterday. Kyle Coleman might be the reason, and someone needs to watch out for her."

Travis interrupted, probably trying to defuse the tension flaring in the room. "Sir, Murphy is no fool. He also has Kristin James's trust."

Well, that was debatable.

Travis fired a pained look at Lucas, like he knew he might be about to cross a line. "Let him listen in."

Had his friend volunteered him to spy on Kristin? Surely not.

Draper eyed Travis, ignoring Lucas. "He can stay close for now, but he'd better be careful. I need to talk to the commander about all of this." He shot Lucas a loaded look and stalked out, clearly expecting Travis to follow.

Travis hesitated. "I'm sorry, man. It was the fastest way I could think of to keep him from ordering you away from her. Somebody's got to have Kristin's back, and her brother's not here to do it." He was gone before Lucas could respond.

Lucas dug his knuckles into his desk. He ought to be grateful Travis had buffered the conversation, but the whole day grated. Too many people in his business, bossing him around.

And Kristin lying to him.

His phone vibrated, and frustration drove him to jerk it from the desk. "Murphy." He shot venom into the greeting, hoping whoever was calling would state their business quickly. If the lunch break wasn't over, he'd change into his PTs and run a ten-miler with a fifty-pound ruck. Still wouldn't blow enough steam.

"Lucas?" Kristin's voice bled through the phone, weighted with something he couldn't measure.

He dropped into his chair and blew out a deep breath laced with exasperation. This was the definition of thin ice. "Everything okay?"

"I'm fine, but…" She exhaled loudly. "My car's missing."

SIX

Oh, how Kristin hated having to call Lucas, but she'd had no choice. She needed someone to run interference with the police, but not in a million years would she tell Casey there had been more mischief at her house. The woman would move into the spare bedroom, and the last thing Kristin needed was an overprotective best friend disrupting her solitude.

She leaned against the window by the front door and watched as Lucas chatted with a police officer on the sidewalk. Rarely did she see him in uniform, occasionally catching glimpses as he went back and forth to work. The close view, his shoulders strong and his stance speaking authority, was more than the fragile distance she held between them could handle.

Maybe she should have called Casey. After all, Casey might have threatened to move in, but that was all she could threaten.

Lucas, with his superhero attitude and all-American army poster-boy self, was a bigger threat.

She was an idiot.

And she was supposed to be angry with him. After

she'd told the alarm company not to notify the police, Lucas had made the call.

True to what she believed, the justice system did what it could, but extra patrols had failed to do anything. When the call from the alarm company came, her first assumption was she'd race home to find her house trashed. But no, whoever had breached the back door had abandoned the house when the alarm went off and gone for the easier take…the classic car housed in the detached garage behind the house.

When Kyle was killed, he'd left Kristin the deep blue '68 Camaro he'd poured most of his money into restoring. After he'd been stationed at Bragg not long before he deployed, he'd started coming around. For the first time since their mother died, he'd been interested in having a sister. Well, he'd hung around her house a bit, helped her finish up some remodeling and stored his car in her garage, usually letting Lacey tag along to do some work, too.

The nights he'd spent working under the hood of that thing held special memories, especially the times when he came alone. No, they'd never talked about their personal lives, never discussed their dad's violence or their mother's death, but they'd shared the same space. Even though it was awkward, that time left Kristin craving a deeper connection with her brother. His car would always represent the healing left unfinished when he died.

When Kristin learned he'd left the car to her, she'd lost her usual iron grip on her emotions, had sat in the front seat for hours, crying for him, for what had never been, for what never would be.

Now his Camaro was gone, the loss a raw wound, like losing Kyle all over again.

And what had she done while her grief was already tearing her in two?

She stared out her living room window at the two men out front, the tall soldier and the equally tall police officer, finishing the report on her missing vehicle.

Yep. What had she done in her fragile state? Called the one man who managed to get inside her head. Turning from the window, she forced herself into the kitchen to take a moment alone before Lucas started asking questions.

She'd grabbed some water when the front door opened and Lucas came in like he belonged, shoving his maroon airborne beret into his leg pocket. "You can stop hiding. The police are gone."

"You make me sound like a fugitive." Kristin stopped at the door of the dining room. In that uniform, Lucas had a way of making the house seem smaller, like his presence filled every corner.

She hated it.

Taking a sip of water to ice her words while she contemplated what to say next, she watched him as he double-checked the locks on her windows, patrolling the room like his duty was to make sure she was safe.

Kristin chewed the inside of her lip, determined not to notice the intensity that seemed to pour off him. She'd called him this one time. It wouldn't happen again. "I have to meet a client in half an hour. Thanks for being the go-between this afternoon."

"Where are you meeting this client?" He stopped staring at the window and met her eyes for the first time since he'd arrived an hour ago. His tone held an edge too sharp for her to grasp.

Kristin's fingers tightened around the water glass. "Two streets over."

"New client or established client?"

Why did this have to turn into a standoff? "New."

"And you're going alone?"

When she nodded, Lucas barked a harsh laugh that bounced off the walls, a sound she'd never heard before. "You don't get it, do you?"

Was he implying she was stupid? Drawing her head back, Kristin sloshed water on her hand, but she ignored the chill. "Don't get what?"

"You're in danger." He took two steps toward her, then stopped like he'd thought twice about getting closer.

He'd better think twice. Reflexes might make her fight. She was pretty sure she could take him out with one swift kick to the chest.

Her gaze drifted to the broad expanse beneath his uniform. Okay, maybe not. "What are you so touchy about, anyway?"

"Listen to me." He downshifted from anger to something that sounded like Animal Control talking down a rabid wolf. "Whatever is going on, this guy doesn't play. He came after you in a public park. I caught somebody in your yard. And now your car's stolen in the middle of the day? That's brazen. Kris, I—"

"Kristin." This was the second time she'd had to correct him. Nobody called her Kris except Casey. The sound of it in a male timbre usually crawled down her spine like a snake. But when Lucas said it...

When Lucas said it, the nickname sounded protected and warm, and that scared her even worse.

"Kristin." He stalked to the front window. "Talk to me. What is so special about that car? This isn't random. It can't be." He gripped the side of the window frame. "You're being targeted. Why?"

It took a second for the words to penetrate, but when they did, they smacked with all the force of the guy who'd tried to tackle her on the trail. This was more than a few strung-together acts. It was stalking, hunting prey. The reality drove home for the first time. She reached blindly for the table, setting the water on it before grabbing the back of a chair. Few things scared her. But someone stalking her the way her father had stalked her mother? Methodically, purposefully... That was the one thing that could knock her legs right out from under her.

Lucas was at her side in an instant. He pulled out the chair and took her by the elbow, easing her into it.

She didn't even have the strength to fight him for treating her like some kind of swooning debutante. She stared at him, unable to form a coherent thought past memories coated in her mother's blood.

The sudden show of weakness drove Lucas's emotions into high gear. He wanted to shield Kristin, to pull her against him and tell her he had this. But he couldn't. There was little he could do until he knew for certain she wasn't knee-deep in whatever had gotten her brother killed. Sure, he was supposed to be watching her, but being a go-between with the police had probably already crossed a line.

He pulled out a chair around the corner of the table, out of reach. If he was close enough to touch her, he would.

She finally looked at him. "Why is somebody coming at me?"

"That's what we have to figure out." He waited for her to buck at the *we*, watching for any sign she was hiding something, that she knew more than she had let on.

Instead, her shoulders slumped and she braced her elbows on the dark wood table. She dropped her head into her hands to knead her temples with her thumbs. "I don't know. I keep running things through my head and can't figure out a reason somebody would do this."

She seemed so certain of her own innocence, so confused by everything going on. Surely this wasn't an act. If it was, the woman deserved an award. "Tell me about the car. Why would someone take it?" He hadn't even known the classic was stored in her garage. He'd never seen her drive it. The deeper they got into this day, the more he realized how little he knew about the woman sitting across from him.

Kristin shrugged and toyed with her water glass, the condensation forming interlocking rings on the table. "It's a '68 Camaro. Meticulously restored. Any fanboy would come after it, and I'm going to guess it's worth some money."

"Who'd you buy it from? Maybe—"

"It was my brother's."

Her brother's. Things were starting to makes sense, even though Lucas didn't want them to. He dug his fingers into his thigh, picturing the cold set of Major Draper's jaw when he'd found out Lucas knew Kristin. Well, the man had implied Lucas could watch out for her. Maybe he could find out the truth about how much she knew.

Questioning her character clawed at him. Nothing good could come out of this. Even if she wasn't involved, proving her brother's guilt would bury her in debris when her family crumbled.

But it had to be done, and he was the only man who could do it. "Let's walk through this." Lucas laced his fingers together on the tabletop. "Someone comes after you, then your brother's car disappears. Do you think that's coincidence?"

Kristin froze, so still Lucas wasn't even sure she was breathing. She flicked a glance at him, then at the table.

The action made his skin cold. What was she hiding? "Tell me."

She swallowed so hard he could see the movement in her throat. Kristin opened her mouth, chewed her lower lip, contemplating before she sighed as though she was giving up. "The man on the trail. He said he wanted to talk about my brother."

Lucas sank in his chair and dropped his head back, staring at the ceiling. "Did you tell the police that?"

"No."

"Why not? Don't you think—"

"I don't know why." Water sloshed on the table as Kristin shoved the glass away. "Things with Kyle were complicated, and I—I don't know."

The flash of anguish that she extinguished as quickly as it appeared almost ripped his heart in two. He hated this. All of it. And he hated most what he had to do next. "Was he into anything illegal? Maybe this guy wants something he thinks Kyle has?" He waited on a knife's edge, aware he was baiting the woman he called his friend. If there was something lower than chewed gum on the bottom of a running shoe, it was probably him right now.

She shoved the chair from the table and stood, ice

in her gaze. "He was my brother. Are you really implying he was a criminal?" Her voice pitched higher. "He's dead. You don't get to accuse a dead man when he can't defend himself."

The force of her anger landed a blow. Lucas moderated his reaction and tried not to respond in kind. Being yelled at had never sat well with him, had landed him extra duty in basic until he'd learned to holster his temper.

He stared at the condensation rings she'd left on the table, counted to ten. Counted to ten again. Didn't speak until he knew he could hold himself together, knew his anger was more at himself for putting her in this position than at her for reacting. "Just trying to see every angle. I want you safe. That's all."

Her head jerked, and her eyes caught his, heating with something like warmth before dropping off the cliff into a flash of fear. "I'm sorry. You're right. I hate it, but you're right." She looked away, then sat and reached for her glass, taking a long drink before she spoke again. "I hope I'd have known. He didn't talk much, was more of a manual-labor kind of guy, but still…if he was pushing drugs or something, I don't know when he'd have had the time or where he'd have kept them. He lived in the barracks, spent a few weekends here in the guest room, kept pretty much to himself. Unless…"

Lucas wanted to jump up and grab her by the shoulders, make her finish that sentence. *Prove to me you're innocent, Kristin. Come on.* "Unless what?" His voice deepened, but he didn't have time to care.

"Gambling? Maybe he got into deep debt. Online, maybe. One of those fantasy sports sites. Or poker. He never borrowed money from me, and he had plenty for the car, so that's unlikely."

Lucas deflated. No answers. None. Only a woman sitting in front of him grieving her brother. Lost. Confused.

Hopefully innocent.

Man, did he ever hope she was innocent. Right now, he wanted to find a way to make her smile in the midst of a world of hurt and fear, but he wouldn't. He couldn't risk tripping into feelings for her, mistaking sympathy for something more. The way his chest felt, he was already in danger.

When he lifted his head, she was watching him, something haunted darkening her blue eyes. "You have to go back to work, and I've got…" She waved her hand toward the front door. "I've got a client."

"Not alone, you don't." Lucas stood and closed the gap between them, trying to assert some authority, trying to make her see she couldn't go to a stranger's house alone, even if it was for work. Not now.

Kristin stiffened, a flicker of panic ghosting her expression, but then she shrugged. "Have it your way." She turned on her heel and disappeared into the living room and up the stairs, leaving Lucas to watch her walk away.

SEVEN

"Thank you, Mrs. Jennings." Kristin offered a wave from the cracked sidewalk, trying all the while not to stick her tongue out at Lucas for being oh so very wrong about her safety.

"I'll see you next week." The older lady held court from a creaky wooden rocker on an equally creaky wooden porch, her nylon wind suit scratching a melody every time she moved. She aimed a finger at Lucas, who stood halfway between the house and the street. "Bring your handsome assistant with you next time, too. And if you bring back that container, I'll make sure to have more cookies ready." She winked and chuckled, brushing carefully curled white hair from her forehead. "Y'all have a nice day."

Kristin threw another wave and met Lucas at the street. She waited until they were a couple of houses away before she unleashed the *I told you so* she'd been holding back since they walked into Mrs. Jennings's house an hour earlier. "Man, Lucas. I'm really glad you came with me. I'm not sure I could have defended myself against an octogenarian."

"Sure. You didn't need me." Laughter twitched the

corner of Lucas's mouth. "She bought a ten-session package from you. I'm pretty sure it's because of me. You're welcome."

"Whatever." Kristin could brush him off, but she wasn't entirely certain his joke wasn't truth. The older woman had fawned all over Lucas, flirting like a nineteen-year-old. She'd even confessed when Lucas was out of earshot that "the boy" was a "breath of fresh air."

Boy. Maybe she'd keep that one in her pocket to bring out the next time the man beside her pulled out his overprotective card.

Popping the lid off the container of chocolate chip cookies, Kristin inhaled the fresh, sweet scent. She pulled one out and it still felt slightly warm, like the treats had come from the oven right before Kristin and Lucas arrived. She held the container out to him. "Here. You want to check them for poison?"

Lucas fell into step beside her and grabbed a cookie, ignoring her snark. "You could have told me your new client was not a male in the fighting-age demographic." He'd run across the street before they left for Mrs. Jennings's and changed into gray basketball shorts and a black T-shirt that showed off the definition he'd built over years in the service. No wonder Mrs. Jennings was smitten.

No need to go down that road. Kristin smirked. Mrs. Jennings could have him.

She bit into the cookie, the outside crisp and the inside gooey. Perfect and totally worth the indulgence. "I didn't know. She sounded younger over the phone. All I knew was she wanted to keep active after surgery and physical therapy. I didn't know it was hip surgery."

"You get that a lot?"

"Occasionally." Kristin sidestepped a root poking through the sidewalk. Her business was a source of pride, the reason she got out of bed every morning. "The bulk of my clients are our age, maybe a little bit older. I do a couple of homeschool groups to keep things from getting monotonous." The little kids were her favorite, so excited and so comically uncoordinated. Their innocence and joy reminded her that the world wasn't all dark.

As the black edges tried to push in, she rolled her shoulders. "Would you have let me come alone even if you'd known? You're scared to let me walk into my backyard, let alone walk three blocks through our neighborhood." She looked over her shoulder and pretended to bite her fingernails, choosing comedy over the truth that his presence took the edge off her anxiety. "Think we're safe, Sergeant?"

"Stop it." The words were all business, his earlier humor gone.

Kristin put the brakes on her sarcasm. Yeah, that had probably pushed things too far. "I'm sorry." She should probably chow on a little bit of crow, even though the cookie tasted better. "And I'm sorry about getting snappy at the house earlier."

"You were stressed, and I started asking questions about your brother. I'd have probably cracked, too."

"I didn't crack." Kristin snapped the lid on the container and popped the rest of the cookie in her mouth, savoring the bite. Downing the whole container would be awesome, but it would wreck her training. The rest of the yummies could go to Casey, who managed to scarf whatever was set in front of her without any ill effects.

She brushed crumbs off on her leggings, wishing she could brush off everything else so easily. "It's not you playing interrogator, although that was annoying." She hip-checked him, then grew serious. "I'm not used to someone watching after me, and I can't decide if it's good or bad."

"Not even your brother? I thought brothers were annoyingly protective of their sisters."

If only their relationship had been that way. The what-never-was singed her heart. "My family was complicated." An understatement if she'd ever spoken one.

"I think you'd be hard-pressed to find a family that isn't." The way he said it hung heavy between them, like he was talking about more than Kyle.

It almost sounded like he knew from experience. "Rough childhood?" Let him answer the questions for once. Kristin preferred to keep her past buried.

"That would be an understatement." He sniffed a bitter laugh. "You don't want to hear my history, though. It's just that. History."

Kristin swept her free hand out to encompass the world around them. Trees were budding early after the mild, snowless North Carolina winter. The air was warm, and the breeze hinted of the unbearable summer to come. Right now, though, the day was one of those perfect ones that blessed them on occasion, mild and beautiful. "I've got nowhere to be, and if you want to talk criminal, spending the afternoon inside on a day like this might fit the definition."

They reached her driveway, but neither of them slowed to turn in. She ought to go inside and tell him he could go on with his day, but something kept her feet moving past her house, and he didn't seem any more inclined to walk away than she did.

That was dangerous, because the conversation was getting more personal than she usually let it.

Lucas shrugged. "Not much to tell. My aunt raised me after my parents took off."

"Took off?" Life would have been a whole lot better if hers had taken off. Maybe her mother and Kyle would still be alive.

"Hard partiers. Crazy hard. I slowed them down. When I was four, they took me to spend the night with my aunt Susan and never came back."

Kristin's heart stuttered. Four. The thought of four-year-old Lucas, with his dark hair and big brown eyes, watching day in and day out for his mommy and daddy to come for him... The image tore through her with physical pain. She wanted to reach for his hand, to comfort him, but that crossed a line they'd both drawn. "I'm sorry."

Lucas smiled. "Don't be. It was one of those God things. My aunt was a better mother than mine could ever be. They terminated their rights, and she adopted me." His expression darkened and he kicked a rock, skittering it along the sidewalk. "Still, it messes with your head when your parents ditch you."

"It messes with your head when they stay, too."

Lucas slowed, but he didn't stop walking. "How so?"

"Well, they..." Kristin shrugged, not willing to hijack his story or to tell hers. "So, what happened after?"

He was silent, the only sound the shuffle of their feet on the uneven sidewalk. It was the first time Lucas had shown vulnerability, a chink in his firmly placed warrior armor. "What happened makes me look bad."

Kristin laughed. "Mrs. Jennings strikes me as a good

judge of character, and she didn't have a problem with how you look on the inside or the outside."

The tense lines around Lucas's mouth faded into a grin. "Wow, James. Who knew you were hiding a sense of humor?" He arched an eyebrow. "Is she the only one who doesn't have a problem with my inside or my outside?" The inflection in the words was deep, hinting that his tone might be joking but his intentions weren't funny.

Was he flirting with her? Kristin popped the top on the cookies again and held them out, desperate for a buffer but not quite sure she wanted one. "I'm sure plenty of people have no problem with your outside."

"I think you called me ruggedly handsome and irresistible." Lucas snagged a cookie and studied it. "In fact, I'm sure you did."

"Don't flatter yourself." She snapped the lid onto the box, embarrassment radiating outward from her stomach. Flattering him was exactly what she'd done. "What could possibly make you look bad, you all-American hero you?"

"Hero?" He sobered quickly. "Sometimes, when abandonment hits, you start searching for love. Everywhere."

"Oh." She heard him loud and clear. Women. And probably a lot of them. The idea of Lucas as that guy, the one her grandmother had so frequently and needlessly warned her about, was surprising enough to tighten her hold on the box of cookies.

Surely his friendship with her had nothing to do with… Her feet wanted to stop walking, but they couldn't. Lucas had never made one questionable move, and there had been plenty of opportunities. She swallowed her questions. "Kyle was that way."

"Yeah, well…" The way he said it told her he knew all about Kyle's ways. "It took Jesus to set me straight."

"Jesus?" Surely he hadn't gone religious on her. "Are you serious?"

"We can search everywhere, but until we go to the source…" He carefully avoided her gaze. "You should come to church with—"

"I'm good." Jesus was nice for some people, if they needed something to lean on. Frankly, she'd done fine without any help.

Lucas started to say something else, then stopped, the two of them ambling along, passing a few houses before he spoke. "Life with my aunt was as good as she could make it."

"What happened to your parents?"

"I have no idea. Right after I joined the army, my mom called all upset, afraid I was going to get blown apart overseas." His chuckle held a bitter edge. "She cared when it could buy her sympathy. Dad never cared. I don't ever remember him not being high." He scanned the sky like he was searching for something. "I never remember him speaking to me at all." He shrugged, straightened his shoulders, acted like all was well. "Last I heard, they were still together, living in Vegas, not really caring what happened to their son. I guess it could have been worse. At least they didn't kill each other."

The lighthearted expression Kristin had worn vanished under a cloud at the exact same moment the sun did, darkening her countenance and the world around them, cloaking both in shadow. Her feet slowed until she'd stopped in the middle of the sidewalk.

Lucas turned to her. "Did I say something wrong?"

"I…" She sighed and stared at him, face almost slack, expression saying something he couldn't decipher. Confusion, maybe, or hurt.

He ran through his last words but couldn't think of anything that would make her stare at him like he'd somehow betrayed her. Maybe he'd shocked her? His story was rough, but it wasn't as rough as some he'd heard from his own soldiers.

It wasn't as rough as the story he'd overheard Kyle Coleman tell one of his buddies. Right about now, he'd gladly lift the sidewalk and crawl under it.

Lucas drew in a sharp breath. He really was lower than old chewing gum. "Kristin, I'm sorry. I wasn't thinking about your family."

"It's…" With slow, deliberate steps, she approached him, staring at the bare branches of a dogwood tree. "So you know?"

Lucas lifted his hand then dropped it to his side. If he touched her, she'd shut down on him faster than he could stop her. "All I know is a little bit I overheard your brother say once." And it had been flippant, like Coleman had detached from the trauma.

"What did he say?" Keeping her eyes straight ahead, Kristin started walking again, like she wanted to hear but didn't want to make contact.

Lucas matched her pace, their shoulders so close he could feel her through her light jacket. In his whole life, he'd never wanted to reach out and take a woman's hand so much. This was the space where he had to tread lightly, because when it came to Kristin James, the road was littered with improvised explosives. "They were both killed the same night."

"He never could believe the truth." She sniffed and

swatted at a low-hanging branch over her head. "Probably his way of coping. He disappeared for years. Some part of me always believed the brother I grew up with was somewhere inside him, waiting to make another appearance. He never was the same, never let me in again."

He fought to keep his voice level, to cover the emotions swamping him in waves. It took a long time before he could say anything. This conversation was treading dangerously close to territory that could prove her innocence or swamp her in guilt. "When did you see him again?"

"Last year, a few months before he deployed, Kyle called me. He was stationed here and found me. Never wanted to talk about what happened, but did want to make things right between us. He was at the house a lot. Spent a few weekends with me, worked on the car out in the garage. I thought…" Her voice cracked and she lifted her chin. "I thought we were getting somewhere. We weren't."

Something about her story jangled alarm bells. What she was saying didn't match up to reality. "So when did he come to Bragg, exactly?" Surely she knew when her brother had moved back to town.

"Y'all deployed last January? He came in October. Last-minute transfer into the unit."

Lucas schooled his face not to show the shock pinging inside his skull. Kyle Coleman came to the unit over a year before they deployed.

What had made him lie to his sister?

They continued in silence, Lucas straining against the questions forming on his tongue. He knew Kristin.

She wasn't done talking, but if he reminded her he was listening, she'd stop talking.

With a harsh sound, she tugged the zipper on her jacket higher. "My parents were…passionate people. They either loved each other madly or they hated each other madly." She shoved her hands into her pockets and hunched her shoulders against a wind only she could feel. "When they loved each other, they forgot Kyle and I existed. When they hated each other… Mom could throw punches faster than my father could. But never at us. My father, on the other hand…" A shudder racked her, but then she straightened her shoulders and lifted her chin as though she could take back the moment of weakness simply by defying it. "Well, my father always aimed for the nearest female target."

Lucas's fists balled. That a man would lay a finger on any woman was unthinkable. But on Kristin? The thought of her own father hurting her made him hot with fury. He wanted to go faster, push harder. Start running until he could outpace the emotions chasing him and erase the images of her in danger from his mind. And at the same time, to stop walking, pull her to him and promise to never let anything so horrible happen to her ever again, to wipe clean what had to be horrible images from her memories.

She didn't seem to notice him and kept talking like she'd forgotten he existed. "Mom figured out she wasn't his only punching bag and it woke her up. She took me and Kyle and moved us from Virginia to here, with her mother."

"He followed." Lucas couldn't help himself. He had to say something, to release the pressure or blow like a fragmentation grenade.

"She got a restraining order. He violated it. Got arrested. Came back. The police didn't scare him."

Oh, man. So much about how she viewed the legal system made sense now. "That's why you don't bother with the police. It's not because you don't trust them. It's because—"

"They can't do anything to someone who's determined. They couldn't stop him from killing my mom. He thought the rest of us were gone because Kyle and my grandmother were out of town. I was supposed to go but I had a project due for school." She hunched her shoulders again. "Mom felt safer with the alarm on. It was monitored. But by the time the cops got there, it was over. He'd killed her, held the knife to my throat, then sliced his wrists."

"What?" Shock ground Lucas's feet to the concrete. He grabbed Kristin's wrist, turning her toward him. "He held a knife on you?"

Her eyes stayed planted firmly on his chest, but she didn't pull away.

Lord, help me know what to do here. Every ounce of the man inside him wanted to shield her from the memories deepening the lines in her forehead. Making that move might push her away forever. He turned his face to the sky, the clear blue of early spring laced by bare tree branches. A knife attack was brutal and personal, fueled by deep hatred and wild emotion. And Kristin hadn't only witnessed it. She'd nearly been a victim.

He'd known she was strong, but how strong had escaped him. She'd survived one of the worst scenarios he could imagine, and she still stood. The way she'd shoved her hands into her pockets and pulled herself into as small a space as possible told him everything, though. She was an armadillo locked in her shell, unwilling to break out. She regretted letting him in.

I have no idea what I'm doing. None. Give me something, God. Anything.

When he dipped his chin again, she was still staring at the logo on his shirt. "Kristin, you survived for a reason." She had to see that, had to know her life had value.

But she didn't lift her head. This wasn't who she was. Kristin James was a chin forward, face the world kind of woman, not the timid creature who stood before him now. He slid one hand to hers and held tight, then ran a finger from her temple to her chin, tilting her face toward his, desperate for her to grasp the strength he knew lay inside her.

Her eyes grazed his neck and lingered on his lips before catching his, the blue so intense it caught him in the chest and stole every breath he'd ever taken.

Travis was right. This thing between them was skating into dangerous territory.

Lucas couldn't care less. In this brief moment while she was willing to make a connection, he fell into the opportunity, searching her face, tracing the determined line of her jaw, skimming to her lips before coming to her eyes to find the flicker of his own thoughts reflected there. He brushed the hair from her forehead, her skin warm beneath his, melting the rest of the world until the two of them stood alone.

As soon as he touched her, she stiffened, her mouth tightening. She pulled away and shook her head like she was coming back from somewhere else, then turned toward her house and started walking.

It took a second for Lucas's body to relax out of its paralysis, to free itself from a moment he wanted to grab with both hands, a moment with Kristin that had rocked him straight through like no time with any other woman ever had.

EIGHT

She was an idiot.

Kristin shoved the gearshift into Park and sat with the engine running, staring at Lucas's gray pickup at Smith Lake's pine needle–strewn dirt lot. She should have known better than to stick to her routine and head out here today. Lucas knew exactly how she trained, and if she was trying to hide from him while he was so insistent on watching her, this had to be the dumbest way possible.

She'd spent half the night staring at the shadows on her ceiling, body tensed and waiting for the house alarm to announce an intruder.

Mind tensed and focused squarely on Lucas Murphy.

The expression on his face yesterday invaded her vision every single time she tried to sleep. She'd known for a while she was harboring the slightest of crushes on him. How could she not? He was tall and built, brown eyed and gorgeous. Coupled with the sense of humor he somehow managed to work in at the right time every time, Lucas Murphy was all the things women dreamed of. She'd even noticed other women looking at him when they were running together. Yeah, Lucas was all that, and she'd known she needed to be careful.

She hadn't realized how truly dangerous he was.

The minute she'd dared to lift her eyes from his chest to look straight at him, every single resolve she'd ever built against relationships dissolved. With her emotions spinning over memories, it had been easy to fall straight into what Lucas offered her, to crave the security of his arms around her.

The feel of his lips on hers.

No. Absolutely not.

She'd shut him out at her front door and tried to keep busy the rest of the day, figuring taxes for her business, scrubbing her already spotless kitchen, working her core until her abs screamed… Nothing had driven Lucas out of her head.

A good trail run might do the trick, but here he was, waiting for her. Protecting her.

She kneaded the steering wheel with both hands. What she ought to do was pull out and go home, crawl into bed and pull the covers high, ignore Lucas and the whole rest of the world for the day…the week…the month. But she'd never been one to run away.

Lucas Murphy was not the man to make her start now.

Kristin twisted the key and turned off the engine with a little too much force.

Shoving out of her SUV, she slammed the door and stalked across the parking area, rapping on his window with her knuckles.

He jerked his head away from his phone and cocked a half grin, then slid out of the truck. "Ready to—"

"What are you doing here?" The best defense? A very strong, very angry offense.

Lucas didn't back away. In fact, he didn't even seem fazed. "Getting ready to hit the trail with you."

"I don't think so. We've never run trails together before. We've always stuck to the neighborhoods around ours." And they didn't need to start running out here together today. This was her happy place, where she came to run the cobwebs away. She needed to clear her head of Lucas, not run side by side with the man. Even standing six feet from him, his presence was overwhelming.

"Kristin, you stuck to your routine. Think about it. If I knew you were headed out here, so does anyone else who's been watching you. After you ripped into that guy's hide the last time, nobody's going to be dumb enough to give you an opening for a repeat performance. They'll sneak up on you and have whatever it is they're after before you even know they're there."

Chill bumps raised along her arms, seeming to ripple even in her stomach. Biting the inside of her mouth, she willed the shudder away, choosing anger instead.

He was right. Turning away from him, she stared at the pine trees whose green needles turned the gray early-morning sky into lace. Oh, how she hated how right he was. Someone wanted something of her brother's, and she was the one link this shadow person had. Well, she'd have to be more vigilant, that was all. It still didn't mean she needed Lucas running alongside her. "I'm fine. I can be on—"

He laid a hand on her shoulder and turned her to face him, but she stared past him at his truck. "Listen to me. I get it. You're strong. Nobody's questioning that. But you're also—"

"A woman?" She jerked the warmth of his hand from her shoulder.

He laughed. "You definitely are, but I wasn't going anywhere near there. I've got combat-ready soldiers who can't throw down an aggressor the way you did the other day." The spark in his eye took on a different glow, one warmer and even more disconcerting. "You're also human. As vulnerable as the next man or woman. You don't have eyes in the back of your head. Be smart. Give a guy a break and let him have your back. I'd do the same thing for Travis if someone came at him the way someone's coming at you."

Kristin puffed air out, sensing her resolve soften and hating herself for it.

"You let me run with you or I dog your heels the whole way. You're not shaking me until this is over and we know who's after you, James. You might as well live with it." The dogged determination in his expression said he wasn't letting this go, even if she did fight him.

Lifting her hands in surrender, Kristin opened the distance between them. Having him beside her was preferable to feeling his presence behind her for the next hour. "Fine, but it's an easy run today." Easy because her shoulder still ached where the dude shoved her into the tree a couple of days ago. Not that she'd ever admit such a weakness to Lucas. Or to anybody else, either.

"Works for me." He jerked a thumb toward the head of the trail. "Let's go. You set the pace."

That was the problem. She knew the pace she wanted to set. Unfortunately for her, her heart was aiming for a whole different rhythm.

* * *

Their feet found a rhythm together, pounding the dirt and pine needles of the trail and laying a backbeat to the sounds of the birds that never left North Carolina. The air was chilly, burning his lungs for the first half mile. It took time, but Lucas relaxed into the tempo, slower than they usually ran together but fast enough for today. If he was guessing right—and he was pretty sure he was—Kristin was suffering the effects of the beating she'd narrowly avoided on this very trail.

He had to hand it to her. After what had happened out here, pretty much every woman in the world would have avoided running alone, and they definitely would have avoided running alone at the scene of the attack. He'd seen grown men have to pull themselves together to go on patrol again after an assault. There was no shame in defense mechanisms.

But Kristin James? She acted like the worst thing in her life was Lucas himself. It tweaked a little, but he really couldn't blame her, not after the way he'd almost kissed her yesterday. When he'd walked her to her house, she'd been quick to silence any further chatter, quicker still to shut the door in his face after she climbed the steps. It wasn't anger, though. It was more like fear. More fear than she'd shown coming out here today, for sure. After what she'd confessed, he had no doubt men were her least favorite people.

Except she didn't seem afraid of the man who'd manhandled her. So what was it about Lucas that sent her packing?

The pounding of their feet took on a sudden, maddening monotony. He had to break the silence or lose his mind. "Did you think of any other reason that guy might have mentioned your brother?" It wasn't an ideal topic, but it was neutral territory with no hint of the kiss they'd nearly shared.

Kristin exhaled loudly. "No. Thought about it all night but...no." She lifted her hands above her head and slowed to a walk. "Hang on a sec."

"Side stitch?" Lucas pulled up the pace and walked beside her.

"Back cramp." She stopped and leaned to the side. "I'm tighter than I thought I was."

So he'd been right. She was hurting and not showing it. "You sure you didn't crack a rib? He slammed you into a tree pretty hard."

"I'm sure." She leaned to the other side then settled into a jog, slower this time. "Lucas?"

"Yeah?" The way she said his name sounded right. She didn't say it often. He kind of wished she'd use it more.

"The army said Kyle was shot and killed." She didn't turn to him but kept her focus on the trail. "He was in your battalion. Were you there?"

The question drove the air from his lungs. He slowed to catch some air, then picked up speed again when her pace didn't slack. Questions like this one were another good reason not to get attached to any female family member.

Maybe that assessment wasn't fair, though. Kyle Coleman may have done a lot of things, but he was still Kristin's brother and she was still grieving, even if she tried to pretend she wasn't. The least Lucas could do was give her an answer.

Lucas swallowed hard, his details probably as sketchy as hers. "I wasn't there. I was on a combat outpost about fifteen miles out from the forward operating base. Kyle was in my platoon for a while, but he…" Yeah. No way was he going to say her brother was such a problem nobody trusted him in combat. "He was on the forward operating base, in headquarters company."

"In the mail room." She sniffed what sounded like a sharp laugh. "You don't have to pull the punch. I was raised in a military town. I know some guys join for the routine stuff and I know others get their butts handed to them when they screw up. Kyle never would have volunteered for mail. He was too much of an adrenaline junkie. He was trouble. I get it. I might not have known him well there at the end, but I knew him well enough."

Lucas glanced her way in time to see her expression darken. Once again, that overpowering urge to shield Kristin kicked in, forcing his feet to pick up the pace before he stopped entirely and gave in. Even though he tried to remind himself, he kept forgetting that though she wasn't a suspected smuggler, she was close to someone who was. "Fair enough."

"What do you know?"

He chewed on the words, unsure what to say. The army had likely told her everything she needed to know, and he couldn't tell her the one new piece of information he had, that Kyle's death had been friendly fire. The question was, did he want to rehash this with her?

Yes, he did. Because then he could be the one to comfort her if she needed it. "He was on guard duty. It's rotational."

"And?"

"It was a clean shot to the head. He never saw it coming." They'd reached the end of the trail, their cars in view through the trees, sunlight glinting off the windshield of his truck. He reached for her and pulled her to a stop, holding her wrist in a loose grip. "It sounds awful, but honestly…"

"I know. That's what the army said, but… I don't know. I was kind of hoping there was something more."

It was a familiar desire. He'd heard it from family members before. The need to know what happened, to process every detail. To hear one thing they didn't know before, one thing that might bring their loved one to life in their minds one more time.

With Kristin, though, there was one more detail, and he was certain CID wouldn't want him leaking the suspicion Kyle was murdered, especially not to the sister who might know more than she let on. "I wish I knew more, Kris."

Her shoulders stiffened, and she pulled her wrist from his grasp. "Kristin."

"I'm sorry." She'd corrected him more than once the past couple of days. "You don't like the nickname?" He tilted his head, trying to catch her eye, but she was staring over his shoulder. "I've heard Casey call you that."

She pressed her lips together. "My dad called me Kris. And it doesn't bother me when Casey says it. It's in a female voice. But when I hear a man say it…" She lifted her eyes and caught his. "I don't know. It scares me when you say it."

"Scares you?" He'd never say it again, would erase it from his vocabulary if it caused her any kind of pain.

Her breath hitched. She opened her mouth and closed it, and a sheen crossed her eyes. "It used to, but when you say it, it sounds like… It sounds safe."

There was a soft vulnerability in the words she'd

never shown him before. She looked at him as though she meant everything, as though she trusted him.

Lucas was done. Forget every warning bell clanging in his head. Forget every stupid mistake Travis had made. Forget every dumb ounce of drama that had gone down in their unit.

This was personal.

He closed the small gap between them and pulled her close like he'd finally admitted he wanted to, wrapped his arms around her, trying to tell her with words that wouldn't come that she was safe, he'd shelter her from the memories of her past and the assaults of the present.

He pressed a kiss to her temple, and she melted against him with a sigh that undid everything inside him. He let his lips trail down her cheek until he found hers, then kissed her softly at first. But when she met him in the kiss, she caught him and drew out all of the feelings he'd been trying to hide from himself almost since the first day he'd seen her.

She met him full bore, winding her arms around his neck and pulling him closer, more relaxed than she'd ever been, giving him something from deep inside that no one else had ever given him. This was different, a rightness he'd never felt before, dissolving the walls he'd built around his own heart, burning away the lie he'd been telling himself. He couldn't punish himself for someone else's mistakes, couldn't take on someone else's lessons as his own.

He was meant for Kristin. It washed over him in a peace like no other, and he let go of everything except her.

She gasped and dropped her hands between them, shoving with all of her strength, pushing him away.

The world rushed in. He might be firmly in his right

mind, but she wasn't, and he might have cut her even deeper. Before he could speak, she backed away. With a wild, hunted look, she turned on her heel and ran for her vehicle like she was afraid he'd chase her, leaving him cold on the trail.

NINE

Kristin rammed a fist into the solid leather of the punching bag and relished the impact shuddering her arm. She whacked it with a right cross then caught it with her left fist for good measure, watching the heavy bag come to center before she retreated and swiped her taped hand over her forehead.

She was either bashing in the head of the guy who'd tried to take her down or kicking her own self in the teeth. She wasn't sure which. The one certainty was the way physical motion sure did her good.

Shaking out her hands, Kristin bounced on her toes, trying to keep warm in the chilled basement. Man, she hated reacting to Lucas. Hated she'd let him kiss her.

She smashed the bag with four quick jabs. She hadn't *let him* do anything. She'd practically kissed him herself. Overwrought with the events of the past few days, exhausted from lack of sleep…there were a whole lot of things Kristin could blame this morning on, but the reality was something totally different.

Kissing Lucas had been about a lot more than an intense week of emotions. The ones that had sucker punched her on the trail were feelings she'd never felt before. Lucas had touched something in her heart no one else had ever come close to. She'd opened herself to him, let him see the Kristin James she hid from everyone else. All because he'd made her feel like emotional intimacy was not only a real thing, but something to crave.

She hated him for it.

Except she didn't.

This was the problem. This intensity was the other side of the same coin, the kind of emotion that had stolen her mother's rationality, the kind of emotion that wrecked lives.

He probably thought she ran because she was scared.

He'd be right.

Coward.

She was definitely scared. Terrified, even. Terrified she'd kiss him again and lose herself forever.

Kristin drove another blow into the bag for good measure then quit for the night, the bag squeaking back and forth in the aftermath of her assault. It had been an hour, and she was done. Her muscles shuddered with fatigue.

Frustration and fear had driven the workout too hard, had intensified the pain in her shoulder blade. With her adrenaline ebbing, an ibuprofen, a shower and bed sounded like the best things in the world, even though decent sleep was probably a fairy tale.

She hauled up the stairs into the kitchen for some water, the old wooden steps creaking beneath her feet. Grasping the edge of the tape on her left hand, Kristin started to unwind it, but a small noise from the front of the house made her pause. It sounded like the old hardwoods on the front porch creaked.

She rewrapped her hand, listening. Could have been

the house settling. Ever since she'd moved in two years ago, there were moments when she was certain she heard footsteps in the hallway, only to realize it was the old house turning in for the night.

Flipping on the light, she was half-ashamed of the way the pushback against the darkness eased her anxiety. The incidents of the past few days had left her skittish, something she never let herself be before. Forget it. She'd faced more than her share of fears and could take care of herself, especially from a few settling boards and creaking floors.

Silence took over, and she ran some water into a glass, hand shaking with muscle fatigue, but when she shut off the tap, she heard it again. Slow. Deliberate. Like footsteps creaking across the porch.

Kristin set the glass on the granite counter and kept her eyes on the sink drain, listening, trying to determine if there was really a problem or if her imagination was taking a walk on the paranoid side. A series of thuds, then the alarm keypad beeped its insistent need for a disarm code.

Someone had opened her front door.

Kristin balled her fist, anger ripping through her. It was one thing to attack her on a trail and think he could manhandle her into whatever it was he'd wanted. It was another to invade her yard and steal her brother's car. But to come into her house? Her sanctuary? The one place she'd built as her safe place? This was a whole other animal entirely.

Clenching and unclenching her fists, muscles aching and skin tightening with a combination of dread and adrenaline, Kristin turned, prepared to burst into the living room to face the danger head-on, hoping against hope whoever had invaded her space was unarmed.

Instead, she found herself faced off against a figure in the doorway leading to the dining room. A tall, broad-shouldered man in jeans and a black sweatshirt was watching her. He watched her with the same dark eyes she'd stared down on the trail. The hard set of his jaw beneath a dark ski mask sent shivers along Kristin's neck.

Something about the way he looked at her said he hadn't forgotten what she'd done to him the first time. Tonight he'd be a much more formidable foe.

With her body drained from her overdone workout, she couldn't hold him off, either. Kristin darted a quick glance toward the door, judging the distance and whether or not she could turn the bolt and get out before he could catch her. Running wasn't her first choice, but she'd be a fool to stand her ground and fight when his expression said he wasn't inclined to show mercy.

His gaze darted after hers, and before she could react, he'd launched himself across the small kitchen, driving Kristin's hip into the edge of the granite counter and whipping her head against the cabinet above. Lights danced across her vision as her entire body absorbed the pain of impact. Before she could even gather herself to fight, the man wrenched her to the floor as the house alarm began to blare.

Crashing onto the hardwood knees first, Kristin pitched forward and cracked her chin on the floor, tasting blood, enduring physical pain like she hadn't felt since she was a teenager...worse, even. Her father had been a brute, but he'd always held something back. This guy wasn't anywhere close to pulling punches. He was all in.

Kristin tensed against another blow and rolled onto

her back to find her attacker standing over her with his fists balled. She drove her foot up, but the angle produced a weak blow that glanced off his thigh.

He lunged at her again, and she rolled to the side, but the narrow space between the cabinets and the stove didn't leave her enough room to get away.

Her awkward position gave her attacker the advantage. He drove a knee into her lower back, shoving her hips against the kitchen counter and pressing her face into the floor, grinding her cheek into the hardwood.

There was no fight left, no good exit.

The man leaned lower, his knee grinding into the small of her back, his breath hot on her face. He cursed and hefted himself up, jerking her to her feet. "Shut off the alarm. Now. Then tell me where Kyle hid everything."

Lucas shoved out the front door and raced across the street as Kristin's burglar alarm fell silent. She'd have words for him if it was a false alarm, but he couldn't take the chance.

He'd risked staying inside tonight as the temperature dropped. She'd warned him away from her after their kiss, before she slammed into her SUV and roared off, leaving him weak-kneed and hating himself for pushing her too far. He'd trusted her house alarm would summon him, but now? Now fear and adrenaline pumped through him.

The story of her mother's murder fresh in his nightmares, Lucas pushed harder. He might already be too late.

The front door stood open, and Lucas barreled through,

stopping in the middle of the small living room to get his bearings, praying Kristin was okay.

A grunt and a thud came from the kitchen, and Lucas's feet pounded the floor as he bolted that way, stopping only long enough to survey the scene.

A man held Kristin against the wall by the alarm keypad, hand pressing against her head with a fury that said he might kill her…if he hadn't already. His back was to Lucas, and he leaned close to Kristin, obviously assessing the situation and trying to decide the best way to finish the mess he'd started.

White-hot anger charged through Lucas, crowding past and present together. Her father had wounded her body and soul. This guy didn't get to do the same. Lucas crossed the room in three strides, grabbed the man's dark shirt and hauled him to his feet, then hurled him away from Kristin.

Her attacker's face smashed into the kitchen cabinet, cracking the thin wood of the door. He roared and staggered to the side, whipping around as Lucas regrouped, prepared to go to battle and win.

Kristin's assailant turned, hostility flashing in his eyes, then fled the kitchen, his feet pounding across the living room floor toward the front door before Lucas could comprehend what had happened.

He'd been expecting a full-on assault, not the enemy's retreat. Lucas followed as far as the door, stopping when he heard an engine race away from a nearby side street. The ensuing silence roared in his ears. Jogging to the kitchen, he reached for his phone, remembering too late it was on the end table next to the couch. A quick survey of the room showed Kristin didn't have a house phone, at least not one in the kitchen.

None of that mattered right now. Before he did anything else, he had to know she was all right, that whoever the man in her house was, he hadn't done permanent damage.

Kristin stood, leaning heavily against the small desk she used as her office. She swept away Lucas's offers of help and punched a code on the alarm keypad to rearm the device.

"Lucas?" She sank against the door and slid to the floor, her voice losing almost all volume. "Where did you come from?"

He dropped to his knees beside her, assessing her injuries as best he could without touching her. Blood streamed from a cut on her cheek. Her fingernails were broken and chipped where she'd clawed at the floor. But she was alert, even if she was still glaring at him like he was responsible for this whole thing.

They could sort it all out later. Right now, he needed to find a phone and get the police, an ambulance, help...

She pushed away from him, scooting sideways, gauging the distance between herself and the door. She opened her mouth, then closed it again, watching him warily as her fingers kneaded her hip and she tried to shake off what appeared to be encroaching shock. Finally, she steadied herself. "I asked what you're doing here." Her voice was stronger, even though pain drew tight lines around her eyes and mouth.

"I heard your alarm go off." He lowered himself so he could see her eye to eye and eased toward her, the same way he'd approach a wounded animal. "I chased off whoever did this to you, but he had a car waiting. Where's your cell phone? I need to call the police and an ambulance. You shut the alarm off too fast for the alarm company to call."

"You beat the guy so bad he needs medical help?"

"The ambulance is for you."

"No."

Even though Kristin James had run from him like he was evil incarnate after they kissed this morning, his feelings hadn't calmed down. All Lucas wanted to do was to make sure nobody hurt her again. Instead, he aimed for tough guy, hoping the act would calm his rattled emotions and shake some sense into her. "Don't be stubborn."

"No. I'll be fine." Kristin shifted painfully and moved to stand, then sank to the floor. "Give me a second."

Two minutes ago, when he'd seen her lying on the floor, he'd thought his heart couldn't hammer any faster. He was wrong. It was triple-timing on him now. She was hurting, and there was nothing he could do about it. "You're going to the hospital."

The look she gave him should have frozen his blood. He'd seen her eyes flash a lot of different emotions, but never one that iced them quite as much as this one.

"You know better," Kristin said. Swiping at her cheek, she seemed surprised to see blood on her fingers. She eased herself to her feet, then headed for the living room. "I said I'd be fine and I meant it. Please… leave me alone."

Well, that wasn't happening. She might hate him for the way he'd lost his mind and kissed her this morning, but she didn't get to pretend she hadn't kissed him back. And she didn't get to brush this off. If she wouldn't let him call an ambulance, then the least he was doing was calling the cops. But they could argue in a minute. Lucas jumped to his feet and followed her. "Where are you going?"

"To get the first-aid kit." She never turned, just kept walking, aiming a finger at the front door as she passed. "There's your way out."

Had she cracked her head when she hit the floor? She was going to go upstairs and act like nothing happened? As far as either of them knew, the bad guys were close by, waiting for Lucas to leave.

If she wouldn't give him a phone, he'd go home while she was upstairs and get his, but he was calling the police, whether she trusted their help or not. She didn't get to put herself in danger like this for any reason, especially when whatever had gotten her brother killed now dogged her. Not when he was more certain with every passing second he didn't want to live in a world without her in it. "Kristin."

"Lucas." She stopped with her foot on the third stair and turned toward him, one hand on the railing. "When are you going to understand I don't need to fall for you?" She turned away and eased her way up the rest of the stairs, the sound of a door slamming the end punctuation on her question.

He stood staring after her, stunned as much as if the guy he'd chased out of her kitchen had socked him square in the nose. She'd cut him as surely as if she'd drawn a knife.

She was feeling the same things he was, so why did she deny it so fiercely?

Honestly, the question ought to be why he bothered to help a woman who didn't want him.

The answer was he was falling for her, too. Harder than he ever should have been.

He tapped his finger against his thigh, then turned on one heel and stalked out the front door.

TEN

The whole house shuddered when Lucas slammed the front door.

Kristin dug her fingers into the edge of the granite counter in the tiny hall bathroom and stared at the mirror, breathing out a sigh she told herself was relief, but she knew better. Deep inside where she refused to acknowledge it, a tiny sliver of something was terrified there was a masked man lurking in the shadows, waiting to invade her space and beat her worse than the time before.

The muscles in her fingers ached from holding on to the counter. Whoever the man was, he might have succeeded in killing her tonight if Lucas hadn't come in. He'd acted as if he wanted to. She could refuse to let herself fall for Lucas and still find herself dead at the hands of a man out of control. A violent tremble started in her middle and radiated through her, the fear tangible and hot.

Whoever this man was, he had walked into her house and thrown her around like a rag doll. Her father had done that, and she'd vowed to be strong enough, brave enough, to never let it happen again.

Tonight, she hadn't been strong enough to fight. Had let herself be ordered into turning off her alarm before taking the punishment again. Had broken in the face of an overwhelming physical force that dredged up her past and slammed her to the ground as certainly as her attacker had.

Kristin leaned heavier on the sink, the weight of emotion pulling her lower. As much as she wanted to pretend this wasn't getting to her, it was. Being attacked on the trail was one thing. Having an intruder invade her home was another.

She pushed away from the counter, jerked the bottom cabinet door open and pulled out a first-aid kit. The alcohol pad she pressed against the cut on her cheek burned enough to make her forget the pain in her hip, but the sting dragged tears with it. She grabbed a bandage, but her fingers were shaking.

Someone had come after her. Had violated her home, bested her and planned to do who knew what if Lucas hadn't arrived. She sank against the wall and slid to the floor, pressing her fingers against her eyes to stop the tears threatening to overwhelm her. What was going on? Who wanted to hurt her and why? She could take care of herself, no doubt, but if he kept coming…if the next time there was more than one…

Nausea pulsed harder. She curled tighter, planting her head between her knees, blood smearing on the fabric of her leggings.

Blood. Her blood. Brought on by a man who had no business being in her house in the first place, no right to lay one hand on her.

Kristin wanted to bolt down the stairs and out the front door, to beg Lucas to stay on her couch, to let him call the police despite her belief it would do no good after what had happened to her mother.

Having to be rescued at all was too much. He'd become her hero, her knight in shining armor. Something she had never needed or wanted.

Except maybe she did.

Tripping headfirst into feelings for Lucas Murphy was one thing. Kissing him was another. Telling him she might be falling for him? Stupid.

Kristin lifted her head, letting anger at her lack of control overtake the fear until even her skin felt hot. She was not a victim, not to her own emotions and not to the man who had damaged her body and spirit. Nobody got to treat her the way the man in her kitchen had. She grabbed the edge of the sink and pulled herself up, then covered the cut on her cheek with a bandage. Grabbing the first-aid kit, she headed downstairs to find a file, deal with her trashed fingernails and ice her hip. She had all night, since sleep probably wasn't going to be her friend. There was no doubt with dark firmly settled in, every little creak in the house would sound exactly like footsteps.

Might actually *be* footsteps.

Halfway down the stairs, she stopped, the sight in her living room surging her heart with something very close to fear, but a whole lot warmer.

Lucas stood in between the front door and the coffee table, sliding a phone into his pocket. He lifted his head before she had a chance to turn away and school her reaction. "I thought you left."

"You should know better." The lines along his face were rigid and spoke of anger, although something in his expression hinted her words had wounded him. "I went home to get my phone and called the police."

She stiffened. It wouldn't do any good. There had been too many of them around already, so many more than she'd ever wanted to face. "I don't—"

"I understand how you feel. But, Kristin, you have to understand…every situation is different. It's safer—"

"Nothing's safe. Haven't you figured that out yet? Having an alarm didn't help me tonight, did it?"

"It brought me."

His low words stopped her, thumped an increasingly familiar rhythm into her heart. One she definitely didn't want him to know about.

Kristin dug her fingers into her hair, and the edges of a broken nail caught with a tearing pain. She winced, then wiped the expression off her face. Her emotions may have whacked her, but she wasn't weak, and Lucas didn't need to start thinking she was.

Still, she was smart enough to know when help was needed. And to know when she was acting like a two-year-old. Pulling her hand from her hair, Kristin pointed to the wing-back chair near the door. "If you're staying, you might as well sit." To be honest, Lucas could pitch a tent in the living room and camp out if he wanted. She was tired of fighting, tired of fending off fear and anger and everything else. She'd had enough physical altercations for one day, and engaging in a verbal one might be the end of her.

She dropped to the couch as far away from him as she could get. He was a temptation, plain and simple. This afternoon had been proof. Distance was best. Pulling a file from the drawer on the end table, Kristin tried to decide which of her nails had taken the worst damage.

Lucas skirted the chair she'd indicated and dropped into the one closest to her, reaching for the file. "Let me—"

She pulled away. If Lucas touched her now, especially in any remotely tender way, she was finished. All of her emotions were closer to the surface than they'd been since she was a teenager, and the cracks were sure to rupture. No, she couldn't. It would open the door to talking about their kiss. About how much he had come to mean to her. The door to friendship would slam shut for sure.

Even the heat of his leg near her knee was enough to remind her of how much more she'd started to want, how she ached for him to touch her, to stand beside her. If something didn't tamp down what he did to her heart, she'd give in to those emotions. Would make the same bad decisions her mother had. Would lose herself and all of her common sense.

It would give Lucas all the power and leave Kristin with nothing. She would never again be the one without the power.

Lucas sat in the chair, his posture straight, as though he were three times more uncomfortable than she was. He watched her work then leaned forward, resting his elbows on his denim-clad knees and lacing his fingers together. "I want to talk about what—"

A knock pounded on the door, and adrenaline jolted her fingers. The police. She'd forgotten them.

Trying to cover her reaction, Kristin shot Lucas a glare, then set her stuff aside and refused to stand. Her knees probably wouldn't hold her. "Well, there are the police you called." Her voice was laced with sarcasm she was too tired to hold back. All her confusion and anger and fear were pouring out in hostility she couldn't fight. "You want to be the one to talk to them or am I allowed to tell them they can leave?" She ignored the hurt on his face and sat staring at him. He'd called them—he could answer the door and deal with them. They wouldn't do anything helpful anyway. How could they? The damage was already done.

"You don't get to tell them to go away." He shoved out of the chair and stalked to the door, his shoes thudding on the hardwood. "Every time I think I understand you…"

Kristin watched his back, muscles tense from the day's abuse. Here she sat while he let the police into her house, the same police who hadn't been able to stop her father from slaughtering her mother.

Somehow, she'd already lost control.

Lucas lay on the sofa and stared at the ceiling, counting the ticks of the wooden clock on the mantel and desperately wishing they'd lull him to sleep.

The police had come and gone, taking Kristin's statements and his before trying unsuccessfully to talk her into a trip to the hospital. They promised to increase patrols around the house, but Kristin had gotten into Lucas's head. Nothing felt like enough. His instincts and all of the events surrounding the past few days said she wasn't safe alone.

The argument they'd had when he'd told her he was bunking on the couch probably should have brought the police right back. She'd actually yelled.

He'd sat in the chair near the couch with crossed arms, refusing to engage in the heated discussion. He'd made his decision, and he wasn't changing his mind. Unless she called the police to kick him out, he wasn't leaving her alone.

Kristin had thrown in the towel and stormed up the stairs, leaving him with no pillow and no blanket.

Well, he'd slept in worse conditions.

The banging and stomping upstairs had stopped a couple of hours ago, and other than the creaks and pops of an old house settling in for the night, there was silence.

Still, Lucas couldn't sleep.

The intensity of Kristin's anger concerned him more than anything else. Her brave front was crumbling. He'd seen soldiers crack under less stress than she'd faced. Kissing her had been a huge mistake, adding confusion to an already complicated situation. He should have known better, and he should have apologized sooner instead of staying away all day. With him knowing his limits and with her facing violence and renewed grief about her brother…

Her brother. Lucas sat up and flipped on the end table lamp. Squinting, he stared at the front door, trying to puzzle out the questions pinging in his head. How did Kristin's brother fit into this whole mess?

Lucas dropped his head against the back of the sofa and stared at the ceiling. When it came to Kyle Coleman, he had to believe Kristin knew her brother best. But by her own admission and his own observation, the dude wasn't a stand-up guy. The way he'd wandered into his sister's life, had lied about how long he'd been in town before he sought her out… Lucas couldn't stop thinking it was all part of some greater plan. Problem was, there were too many missing pieces to form a whole picture.

If Kyle Coleman really was involved in trafficking

stolen antiquities, Kristin was going to pay the price in the end, especially if Lucas didn't find a way to prove she wasn't involved. Even Travis had grown insistent when they'd spoken earlier. "Find a way to prove she's not involved before CID decides she is."

Lucas sank lower into the cushions and closed his eyes. *God, I have no idea what to do here. There's not a map for this. You've planted me in a situation where I'm supposed to help this woman, and I've messed up everything I've touched.*

He studied a fine crack in the ceiling, his thoughts tumbling over one another.

Somehow, he'd become the one person who could make inroads into whatever had led to Kyle Coleman's murder. Since coincidences didn't exist, he knew he was exactly where he was supposed to be, whether he wanted to be here or not, whether he knew why or not.

The sure thing was he wouldn't be sleeping tonight. He pulled his phone off the coffee table and pressed the screen.

Dead.

That was all he needed. A dead cell when anything could happen. Well, Kristin had the same phone as he did, and last he remembered, her cable was attached to the computer in the kitchen. And coffee was in the kitchen. If he was going to be awake, he might as well make it count for something.

With a hefty groan, Lucas shoved off the couch and slipped into the kitchen, trying to tread lightly in his socks. He'd traded his jeans and sweatshirt for track pants and a T-shirt. The change wasn't helping him relax. He was as antsy and ready to roll as he was when he was geared up in full battle rattle.

Dragging a hand down his face, where a day's growth scrubbed his palm, Lucas searched cabinets and drawers until he found the coffee, then scooped it into the machine. The coffeemaker hissed, and coffee dribbled out, warming the air with the familiar scent of the strong brew.

Once it started brewing, he went to the small desk by the back door where a laptop sat, the lone item on the pristine surface.

He surveyed the hardwood floor and the granite counters, noticing again how everything had purpose and a place. It was like Kristin laid her life out in a particular order and kept it just so.

Which made sense, considering the things she'd told him about her childhood.

Before he'd kissed her and wrecked her trust.

Scrubbing at the corner of his eye, Lucas turned toward the desk again and slipped the free end of the charger into his phone.

The laptop screen flickered to life.

Lucas stepped back and glanced at the door that led toward the rest of the house, then to the machine, Travis's voice echoing in his head. *Find a way to prove she's not involved before CID decides she is.*

He reached a hand toward the computer, his pulse double-timing at what he was contemplating. Could he really search for clues as to why she was being hunted and what her brother had to do with it? A way to stop this madness before Kristin was hurt again...or killed?

He eased closer as though the machine was a camel spider ready to leap, then stared at it, unsure what to do.

Was he the kind of guy who could invade her privacy, even though her brother could have dropped some sort of clue in an email that might save her life?

Lucas eyed the machine, which had opened to the mail program. Several windows sat open, various emails from Kyle. She'd been rereading her brother's emails, probably looking for anything to indicate why his name was coming up in these attacks. He slid into the seat, gut twisting.

The coffee smelled strong enough to wake the dead, every creak of the chair a rifle shot in the silence. If she caught him…

If she caught him, kissing her would no longer be the worst thing he'd done.

All he needed was proof she wasn't involved. Her brother's emails were mostly brief responses to long, conversational emails she'd sent him. Coleman's words were generic, the tone of a man answering an acquaintance rather than his sister. There was no pattern, nothing to indicate he'd ever even hinted to Kristin what he was involved in.

Relief loosened Lucas's tight shoulders. So far, everything confirmed what he already believed about Kristin. She wasn't involved. But her innocence didn't bring him any closer to answers about her brother.

Lucas sat back and skimmed, then stared at the wall above the computer. Coleman had been on the larger forward operating base with near-constant access to a computer, yet he'd managed to email his sister a handful of times, and only in response to her queries. He skimmed the newer emails listed along the side of the screen, trying to see if he'd missed anything.

Until he stumbled on one from about a month ago.

One that contained his own name in the subject line. From Casey.

His heartbeat drummed faster, adrenaline surging

into his system. He'd met Casey around the time the email was sent, and a subject line like *That Lucas guy* indicated she'd had something to say about the meeting.

It was one bad thing to read Kristin's open emails in an attempt to exonerate her. It was a whole other horrible action to snoop in her private emails to learn her thoughts on their relationship.

He tapped the desk, debating his next move and how much of an idiot he wanted to be. Once the email was opened, he could never undo it.

Lucas scanned the folders on the sides of the page— email strings from clients, based on the subjects. Still, Casey's seemed to glow in his peripheral vision, calling him to see what she'd said and if Kristin had replied.

Until he caught sight of another folder halfway down the list.

Lucas.

A folder that could only be filled with emails from him. Kristin, who kept no clutter, held on to nothing sentimental, had saved his emails.

He pressed his lips together, refusing to give in to the temptation to peek as frustration washed through him. There was nothing open on the laptop to indicate a way to end this nightmare. Nothing to help. And no way would he violate her privacy by digging deeper. He had nothing to go on.

Only his emails, and more confusion than he'd had when he started.

ELEVEN

Kristin leaned against the kitchen counter and watched fairy dust dance in the light that slanted in from the windows and left bright squares on the hardwood. She'd spent the morning unsuccessfully stretching out the pain from last night's altercation before she headed down the stairs and stood in the doorway of the kitchen, inhaling and exhaling in a rhythm designed to ward off the certainty she never wanted to cross the threshold again. The certainty she never wanted to see the place where she'd been bested and Lucas Murphy had become her hero.

The warm coffee mug resting against her palms soothed some of the stress. Sure, some of her colleagues hated the stuff, claimed it was all kinds of unhealthy and tea was the thing, but there was something about coffee that felt so much more indulgent than tea, like a guilty pleasure, a comfort she'd never felt anywhere else.

Except lately, with Lucas Murphy.

He'd left early, not long after first light, probably headed to church. Every Friday when they ran together, he'd ask if she wanted to go with him. And every Friday, she said no. In the chaos of this week, he hadn't asked.

In the chaos of this week, she might have said yes.

It was a good thing he'd left.

She shifted her hip on the counter, trying to avoid the bruise that had created an ugly reflection in the mirror this morning. One more reminder this was real. It became more painfully real with each encounter with the man who wanted…

She sighed. He still hadn't said what, other than that Kyle had it.

Her plan for the day had been simple. Stretch, get a shower and then face the kitchen. She'd climbed the first hurdle and was in the room. Although standing in this spot tensed everything her earlier stretches had loosened, she could slowly sense the power returning. This was her home. Nobody got to scare her out of it.

Kristin had thought she'd spend the rest of her morning cleaning blood off the floor, but apparently Lucas hadn't slept last night. The hardwood was spotless, as good as if she'd scrubbed it herself. A smile wrapped around her mug as she sipped her coffee. He knew she was a hyperorganized freak.

The smile dipped. Maybe he knew her too well. How had that happened? Her whole life, she'd managed to keep her distance. Lucas Murphy had kicked her walls apart with his combat boots. She'd kissed him.

And she wanted to kiss him again. To spend every day knowing she had the right to kiss him whenever she wanted, to feel the safety of knowing he was hers and he was watching over her. As much as she'd fought the idea of him bunking on the couch last night, it was the first solid night's rest she'd had in…

Ever.

Kristin dropped her head against the cabinet and stared hard at the ceiling.

With a groan, Kristin shoved herself away from the counter and refilled her mug. Thinking about Lucas all day was going to do nothing but make the situation worse. Distance. She had to keep her distance and somehow cool off her emotions. The trick was finding something to overtake her thoughts until nothing else could filter in.

Taxes. Nothing put the kibosh on feelings like figuring out how much money she owed Uncle Sam. Might as well start now. If everything went her way, the job would take all day and leave her too mentally drained to think tonight.

Easing into the chair at the small desk, Kristin settled her coffee mug on the warmer and ran her finger across the track pad to wake the machine.

She leaned over to pull a file from the two-drawer oak cabinet next to her. The movement brought screaming protest from every muscle in her body. This was more than getting tossed around like an empty flour sack last night. This was the way-too-hard workout she'd attacked yesterday afternoon trying to work Lucas out of her mind. If she wasn't careful, he'd wreck every bit of her, starting with her heart.

Determined to shove Lucas out of her mind, Kristin flipped open the file then glanced at the computer screen.

Something was wrong.

A device removal warning sat in the middle of the screen. Her forehead wrinkled. She'd used her laptop since the last time she'd plugged her phone into it, so it couldn't be hers. The warning hadn't been there yesterday afternoon. So who had connected a phone to her computer last night?

Lucas.

Kristin exhaled through pursed lips. Maybe…maybe he had needed to charge his phone. Or maybe he'd downloaded something. From her personal machine. Without her permission.

Anger unleashed from somewhere in her core and pounded in her temples.

She stood, slamming the laptop shut, letting anger wash over hurt and betrayal in bitter waves. No matter what he'd said…no matter that he'd kissed her…he'd betrayed her.

And she was going to find out why.

Lucas grabbed his Bible from the passenger seat and slammed the truck door. Maybe he should have stayed home, but he had a feeling God would have chased him all day if he had.

Knowing a patrol car would be keeping close to the neighborhood had freed him to head to the chapel on post. Since he'd started going to church a few years ago, no message had ever made him so uncomfortable. Sure, worship had been awesome, but the instant Chaplain Freemont opened his mouth to speak, Lucas felt certain the man had been following him around all week and somehow reading his thoughts on a big ol' whiteboard. The man had addressed all of Lucas's fears and doubts, all the things he'd held on to since they left for deployment. *Your walk with Christ doesn't change because someone else hurts you.*

The weight of the words was palpable. No, Travis hadn't hurt him, hadn't purposely set out to hurt anybody, even though the ripple effect had nearly washed Lucas and half the company overboard. Travis had owned up to his mistakes and wasn't the man he used to be, and Lucas couldn't walk that walk for him.

Just like he wasn't meant to bear the repercussions. Just because Travis had royally messed everything up in his own life, it didn't mean Lucas would make the same mistakes. It didn't mean things between him and Kristin couldn't work out.

But first, she had to deal with her own issues and hopefully forgive him for the things he'd done.

That kiss he'd shared with Kristin sure made him want more. Somehow, she'd tapped into parts of his heart he'd never released before.

Leaning against the truck, he eyed Kristin's front door. He should tell her what he'd done. Reading those emails from her brother had weighed on him all morning. He'd violated her privacy, and for no good reason. Sure, he'd been searching for information to prove Coleman's guilt and Kristin's innocence, but halfway through church Lucas put expression to the thing that had nagged him the most the night before…he'd also been relieved to see there was no indication someone in her life had broken through the wall she'd built around her heart.

He hated to admit the relief he'd felt when there hadn't been one personal email from a man or when he'd discovered the folder with his name on it. Somehow, it felt like he'd gained an advantage over her, like he had read her diary and knew her secrets. All of that made him feel even worse now, when he was starting to think maybe, just maybe, God wasn't going to make him live his whole life alone. That maybe, just maybe, Kristin James might be a bigger part of his future than he'd ever dreamed.

Which was a stupid idea. They were friends. That was all. Still, he couldn't deny that something more was happening between them. Something he wasn't quite ready to embrace or push away. Just thinking about it made him feel like he was trapped in a flat spin without a parachute.

The only certainty? He had to make right what he'd done by spying on her personal life, even if he hadn't done the digging on his own.

Lucas laid his Bible on the hood of the truck. He was going over there. Now.

"Don't even think about it."

The voice from the porch, harsh and angry, whirled Lucas around, ready to fight.

But it was Kristin who stood from the chair on his front porch. She stormed down the steps in jeans and an oversize sweater that slouched off one shoulder, making her appear casual and fun.

Except her face was a hurricane, and the fury of the storm was directed straight at Lucas.

He almost backed away. Almost. Retreat would tip the advantage toward her, and with her in this mood, an advantage could be trouble. He started to say something—what, he had no idea—but she beat him to the words.

"Who do you think you are?" She stalked up the sidewalk and stood four feet from him, out of reach.

"What?" She was angry. That he'd kissed her? Insisted on protecting her last night? Or had she figured out—

"My computer. My files. My privacy. Mine, Lucas." She advanced and rammed a finger into his chest. "What did you download off of my laptop? What were you looking for?"

So she did know. His apology evaporated, but he grabbed at what was left and tried anyway. "Kristin, I'm sorry."

"Oh, stop. Just…stop talking." The words dripped disgust as Kristin stalked to the porch before she turned and pinned him with a fiery gaze. "I trusted you. More than I should have. More than I've ever trusted anybody. And you? You took advantage of me."

She'd trusted him? A sick wave crashed in his middle. She'd trusted him, and he'd taken that precious gift and thrown it into the garbage. He had to tell her why. No one had sworn him to secrecy. She had to know, or she'd never trust him again. "It's your brother."

Her eyes widened, and she threw both hands into the air. "My brother is dead. Gone. All of a sudden, everyone wants to know about him. That man? He keeps asking. And you?" She stopped stone cold, like she was frozen in time. "You…you're not…working with the guy who's after me, are you?"

"Haven't we been down this road before?" He reached for her, wanting to reassure her he was the safest place she could be, but she evaded him, eyeing Lucas like he was a wild boar about to charge. "No. I don't even know who he is." He pulled in a deep breath and held it. No, he hadn't been told not to say anything, but the order was implied, and he was about to violate it big-time. "But I do know your brother is being investigated."

"What?" The word was low, like the silent pullback of a pistol's hammer before it fired.

Lucas focused on the front door behind her. He couldn't look at her while he trashed what was left of her relationship with Kyle. "They think he was involved in running stolen Iraqi antiquities to the States, that he used his position in the mail room to smuggle items out."

He shifted his gaze in time to see her catch the implication of his words. "My brother was not a criminal. Yeah, he struggled, but he changed. He was killed by a sniper on guard duty. You told me yourself. Why on earth would you be digging through my computer if it's my brother who's…" The incredulous anger that swept her expression chilled the air between them. "You think I'm involved."

"I don't." He held up two hands, hating the way it made him seem like he was surrendering but knowing there was no other way to talk her down. "I saw the emails on your laptop when I plugged my phone in to charge. I admit it, and I'm sorry. I read what was open, trying to find a way to prove you aren't involved so when the question does—"

"I'm not involved."

"I know, but you coming to the company to drop off a package to one of my soldiers caught the attention of CID. If you're not a suspect now…well, Kristin, you'd better hope Specialist Lacey isn't a part of this, or they will look at you. Hard."

She balled her fists at her sides. "Kyle mailed Brandon Lacey a present for his mother. You can check."

"I'm sure CID already has." He walked toward her, desperate to mend this tear between them, to have a place in her life again. "Believe me. I know you're not involved in anything your brother might have done."

"He didn't do anything." She aimed a finger at his chest. "But you violated my privacy. After you kissed me. You asked everything of me." She stalked closer and leaned into his personal space, bringing the scent of oranges with her. "It's a good thing I didn't give you my heart. Stay away from me, Sergeant Murphy. Far away. Or I'll test how fast the police can get to my house when I call them on you." Shoving him aside, she marched down the driveway and was across the street before he realized he was staring after her with his mouth hanging open.

He started to follow, then stopped. In her mood, she'd never hear a word he said. Not that Lucas could blame her. He'd done everything wrong. Had closed himself off. Had kept the truth to himself. Had kissed her.

You asked everything of me. The words punched Lucas in the throat. Kristin was not a woman to kiss a man on a whim. Lucas wasn't a man to kiss a woman for fun. But she couldn't know that. The way she saw it, he'd used her, and with her history, this wasn't something she was going to get over easily.

Deciding his drive-through burger on the way home had been a really, really bad idea, Lucas swiped his Bible from the hood of his truck and climbed to the porch. There had to be a way to make this right, but he had no idea what. Although he'd tried to protect Kristin James from harm, he'd been the one to cause her the most pain.

He needed a run. A long one. Until he dropped on some side street where no one could find him.

Shoving his key in the lock, Lucas pushed the front door open then stopped, his Bible hanging loosely from his fingers. He sagged against the door frame and stared at the destruction that had been his home.

The house was trashed. Couch cushions scattered and sliced open, holes in the drywall, slashes in the kitchen vinyl, grease smeared across the carpet…

This wasn't a robbery. This was a message, and words weren't necessary to convey the threat. *Stay away from Kristin James.*

TWELVE

"Okay, I love a good latte as much as the next girl, but what's this all about?" Casey stopped beside Kristin's table at the funky little coffee shop downtown and plunked her cup down. "And you didn't have to pay for my coffee ahead of time. What's going on?"

"I called you, I paid for you. Get over it." It always made Casey light up when somebody did something for her, so Kristin did it every chance she got. "And why are you asking so many questions, anyway? You were probably curled up on your couch with your sudoku and inferior coffee. I saved you with my need for the good stuff." Well, that was about a third of the story. The rest was she didn't want Lucas to arrive at her door with another apology. Kristin wasn't ready to forgive him. Besides, the vintage concert posters and album covers at the back of the small space blended with the brightly painted walls to drive away the March funk that added to her inner turmoil.

"Well, you're right about one thing. I'll turn cartwheels on Hay Street if it will get me out of cleaning, and you know I never turn down a berry-rama. Cherry and raspberry in my coffee sounds so wrong but it's so right." Casey grinned and shed her jacket, then slung it over the chair beside her and stared at Kristin for a long time, her smile fading. She started to say something, then stopped and seemed to reconsider as she slid into her seat. "Thanks for the invite, but I'm going to ask again…what's going on?"

"I don't even know where to start." It sounded like a stall tactic, but it wasn't. Kristin had thought she wanted to spill her hurt and anger to her best friend, but the plan was a whole lot better in theory than in practice. Now that Casey was sitting across from her, Kristin didn't want to think about it anymore, let alone talk about it. She sat back in her neon green chair and rolled an orange between her palms. "Never mind."

Casey eased to the edge of her seat and tipped her head toward the fruit Kristin held. "You brought oranges with you? How many of those have you had today?"

"Not sure."

"You're the only person I know who stress eats citrus. You might want to slow down. You're either going to trash your mouth or give yourself some wicked heartburn, especially if you're chasing it with espresso."

Kristin stopped palming the orange and held the fruit for a closer look. Casey was probably right. Leaning forward to thunk the fruit on the table, she reconsidered keeping her mouth shut. "I needed some company, if that's all right with you?"

"Really? You've fought me all week on hanging out at your house to give you backup. You've fought Lucas, too. Since when do you need a babysitter?" If Casey slid any closer to the edge of the chair, she'd slide under the table to the concrete floor. "No, wait. First, you can tell me how you got the cut on your face and if this moment of uncharacteristic behavior has anything to do with it." When Kristin grazed the wound with her fingers, Casey's mouth tightened. "Yeah, I can see it. The whole world can see it. It's a giant billboard for a fistfight on your face. Who did you tangle with this time, and please tell me it wasn't Lucas."

"Really?" Despite the dull throbbing in her cheek, Kristin had forgotten about the visible reminder of last night's insanity. "Lucas would never hurt me." *At least not physically.* "I had another visitor last night." One who had asked specifically where her brother had hidden something. The oranges she'd binged on earlier roiled and tossed. Lucas couldn't be right about Kyle, could he?

"What?" Casey rocketed from the chair and paced the width of the narrow room before she turned around, her face thunder. "Who?"

Behind the counter, the barista eyed the duo, then turned to help a young couple who stood by the counter. The place was quiet for a Sunday afternoon, but even a small audience was too much.

Kristin pointed to a chair. "Sit. If you make a scene, we're done talking."

"Fine." Casey huffed and dropped into her chair again. "But you're telling me the whole story, Kris. No holding back."

This was the price she paid for having a friend who knew her better than anybody. Except Lucas. He had the uncanny ability to read her even better than Casey could.

Kristin brushed off the heaviness that came with thoughts of Lucas. Not knowing what to do about the way she'd let him into her heart stirred her almost as much as the story she was about to tell Casey. "It was the same guy as before. He came in after I finished working out. If I hadn't burned myself out on the punching bag, I'd have had him, but he got the advantage. Lucas heard the alarm and…" She shrugged like it was nothing, but a spike of fear pierced her. What if she hadn't set the alarm? Or Lucas hadn't heard it? She wanted to drop her head in her hands, but doing so would tip Casey off in an instant.

"Tell me you called the cops."

"Lucas did."

Casey stared at something in the far corner of the shop, her thoughts skimming across her face. The lines around her eyes deepened as she looked at Kristin. "You didn't recognize the guy?"

"No."

"Kris, you have to do something." Casey's voice held a pleading warble Kristin had never heard before. "You can't keep this up. One of these times, whoever this is, he's going to get the drop on you, and Lucas won't be around to save you."

I don't want Lucas to save me. As much as Kristin tried to shove the denial out, the words stuck in her throat. What if she couldn't do this alone? What if she needed Lucas more than she ever wanted to?

"I don't want to get a phone call in the middle of the night that my best friend is…" Casey laid her hand on Kristin's bowed head. "Let me stay with you."

Pulling away, Kristin straightened and crossed her arms, raising the last of her inner reserves. "Put you in the line of fire? No. Lucas stayed on the couch last night, but he won't be doing that again."

"Why not?"

"Because he went through my computer." *And because he kissed me.* But she wouldn't be telling Casey about the kiss. It was humiliating after the way he'd betrayed her.

The metal chair legs protested against the cement floor as Casey slid away from the table. She stared at the ceiling for a long time, as though she were searching for answers in the textured paint. "Why would he dig through your computer?"

Oh, where to start? Kristin puffed out her cheeks and reached for the orange again, squeezing it gently. She'd crush the thing right here, but cleaning sticky juice out of her jeans was a task she wasn't up to handling. "The army thinks Kyle was smuggling stolen Iraqi artifacts."

"Oh. Wow." Casey lifted her head. "You're kidding."

"Lucas claims he was searching for proof I'm not involved, but you know Kyle couldn't have been, either." Kristin dropped the orange, and it rolled under the table. She didn't bother to pick it up. "This is my brother we're talking about. My brother, who finally tried to make it right, who…" Who'd been at the center of every attack.

"Who I always told you was shady." Casey held up her hand, her palm a barrier to Kristin's arguments. "You said yourself he acted like he was hiding something, and he never would let you in. If you tell yourself the truth, you were frustrated with him almost constantly."

"I remember, but he's dead."

"Dead doesn't make you a good person."

Kristin propped her elbows on the table and kneaded her temples with her index fingers. "I don't want to talk about this."

"Kyle had a lot of money you couldn't account for. Money he sank into his car." Casey leaned across the table and tapped Kristin's forehead. "The missing car."

Kristin groaned. It physically hurt to think the things she was thinking. Had her brother been involved in something bad enough to get him killed? Had he been at her house not because he wanted to reconcile, but because he wanted to use her for...what? She wrapped her arms around her aching stomach. Yeah, she definitely should have laid off the oranges. "The guy...last night. He asked where Kyle 'hid everything.'"

Casey sighed. "Kris, I hate to ask you this, but... what if Lucas is right?"

"Then I'm a dead woman, because I have no idea how to give this man what he wants."

THIRTEEN

Lucas shoved his phone into his hip pocket and walked into the living room, dreading the sight of the vandalism that still jarred him hours later. The call to his landlord had been tough, and thankfully it was over. Going through everything with the police had taken a huge amount of time, and daylight was fading fast.

Near the shredded couch, Travis tossed a rag into a black trash bag and sat back on his heels. "So, yeah, grease really doesn't come out of carpet easily. Or at all." He swiped his hand across his forehead and stretched toward the couch to grab another rag. "What did the landlord tell you?"

"He's calling his insurance company and they'll send out appraisers. Really, what could he say?" Lucas leaned against the door frame and surveyed the damage. Even with all the work they'd put in since the police left, not much looked different. They'd cleaned the mess as best they could, but nothing was going to get the grease out of the carpets or the holes out of the walls.

The furniture was in position, though most of it was unusable. His next call would be to his renter's insurance company to see what he could get for replacements.

Nothing they'd done in the past couple of hours had helped dampen Lucas's anger. Whoever was behind this thought he'd leave Kristin to them, that he'd scare easily because they'd damaged his stuff.

His shoulders tightened. No. Whoever trashed his house had poked the bear and faced a bigger problem than they'd ever had before. Right now, he was ready to drive to post and interrogate every one of the men in the battalion until somebody talked, because if CID was right and one of them was behind this—

"Hey, brother. Slow your roll."

Lucas's head snapped up, and he caught Travis looking right at him, his expression somewhere between amusement and concern. "Slow my roll? What are you talking about?"

"You're furious. It's pouring off you in waves. Your face is so tight, one of your blood vessels is liable to pop. You can't go at this like a vigilante. You do that, and you'll get yourself and Kristin both killed."

Travis was right. Whatever Lucas felt, he still had to temper his actions with calmer emotions, whether he wanted to or not.

"Besides, while you were on the phone with your landlord, I called Major Draper with CID. He's already on it. Let the system work."

"The system's not doing much for us so far, is it?" Really, things were getting worse, not better. He was beginning to understand Kristin's reasoning.

"The system might work slowly, but it does work. They've got eyes on the guys acting suspicious. They'll know if anybody shows up to formation with grease under their fingernails." He wagged his fingers in front of his face. "Besides me, of course."

The grin Lucas shot him was halfhearted at best, but it did ease the stress a little bit.

Travis seemed pretty proud of himself as he returned to scrubbing a spot the size of a dinner plate. "And listen... the guys in our company? They are still our guys, still our brothers. You cannot go around interrogating all of them and suspecting them of being criminals." He stopped working. "It will tear the unit apart when the wound I cut isn't even healed all the way yet."

Travis seemed to have found peace with his past, and he was right. There was a special bond in the military, but once someone started pulling at threads, things could fall apart, especially if it was leadership ripping the seams. They'd seen that firsthand. Lucas had to pull himself together or risk tearing the company apart once again. "Do you have to be right all of the time?"

"Pretty much."

"Fine." Lucas dragged his hand down his face. "We really ought to throw in the towel here."

"Literally?"

"Literally. We'll grab dinner and I'll buy an air mattress." Whoever had hit his house had trashed everything, even slicing his mattress open. It was definitely a message, one that made him angrier the longer he stood and stared at it.

"What happened here?"

Lucas rooted into place at the sound of Kristin's voice. Taking a second to prep himself for the sight of her, he shot Travis a silent question then turned toward the front door, unsure how this meeting was about to play out.

Silhouetted by the late-afternoon sun, Kristin stood in the doorway with Casey close behind.

And yes, Lucas was a goner. Having her walk into the midst of the chaos—even if she was still mad at him—ran a charge through him that reminded him of what was important.

It wasn't any of his stuff. Losing her to the bad guys was not an option. Even if she walked away in the end and never spoke to him again, at least he'd know she was alive and safe.

These shadow people could throw their worst at him. He wasn't going to back off until this was all over.

Even if she didn't want his help.

She stepped over the threshold like she was coming straight for him, then stopped and eyed him from head to toe. "Are you okay? I wasn't home and we came back and saw—"

He waved a hand, pretending a nonchalance he didn't feel under her scrutiny. "I'm fine. It happened while I was at church."

"This morning?" Her voice inched up a couple of notches.

He knew what she was thinking. This morning. In broad daylight. While she was directly across the street, totally unaware.

All Lucas wanted was to sweep the fear from her expression, but the last time he'd touched her, he'd kissed her. After her rant on his front lawn this morning, he wasn't going anywhere near where he could feel her, smell her...

The rest of the room fell away. His entire focus lay on the woman standing ten feet from him. Too close... yet too far. "Nobody's hurt, so it's all good. Insurance will handle everything. It'll be a pain, but it'll all be fixed. Eventually."

"Tell you what." Travis planted his hands on his knees and stood, then dropped a cleaning rag onto the couch. He aimed a finger at Casey, who still stood in the doorway. "What's your name?"

Lucas pulled out of his stupor in time to catch Kristin wearing an expression that had to match his own. She arched an eyebrow but said nothing.

The other woman glanced at Kristin and almost shrank a little before she answered. "Casey." She suddenly stepped forward, her expression issuing a challenge Lucas couldn't quite read.

"Casey, I'm Travis. Nice to meet you. What say you and I go find Lucas an air mattress and bring back a pizza." He patted his stomach with both hands. "Lucas has had me working like a private in basic training and I'm starved."

It seemed to take a second for the question to register and for the slight shock to clear from her expression. "Okay, Travis. I see what you're about." She threw a wave and turned for the door. "See you guys later."

Lucas's muscles stiffened. He knew his friend wasn't the man he used to be, but this was the first time he'd given any indication he'd noticed a woman since that whole mess at the company went down. "Travis…"

Travis gave him a nod over his shoulder, a silent *I'm okay.*

Lucas had to trust he was, realize when God whacked him upside the head at church this morning, it wasn't all about Kristin, but about being Travis's friend, not his father.

Kristin sucked her tongue against her top teeth and

turned from the door. "You know what happened, don't you?"

"Travis thinks Casey's cute?"

Her eyebrows wrinkled. Kristin was cuter than Casey could ever dream of being. "No." She drew the word out and pointed her finger back and forth between them. "We were left alone to work out our differences."

Through the front window, Lucas watched Travis's blue pickup back out of the driveway. "I see. So we're supposed to hug it out?"

"Don't push it."

He bit down on a grin. "Talk it out?"

"Looks like it." Kristin made a slow circle and seemed to decide the one decent place to sit was the coffee table. She settled onto it, leaving enough room for Lucas to sit beside her.

He'd take what he could get. Easing to the makeshift seat, he kept a good space between them. Still, Kristin was close enough for him to feel her warmth. Yep. He was still close enough to get burned.

She took in the damage to his home, lingering on a large hole in the drywall by the front door. "Was this because of Kyle?"

"I don't know for sure, but I think that would be an educated guess."

"You can almost read it in the air." She splayed her hands in front of her like she was framing a billboard. "Stay away from Kristin James."

He imitated her hand motion and intonation. "Not going to do it."

She chuckled low, then bumped her elbow with his. "I'm sorry about this morning. I'm sure the neighbors think I've lost my mind."

"I'm sure they're thinking worse things because, you know, the cops pulled in right after you left."

"Oh, no." Groaning, Kristin dropped her head into her hands. "I didn't think about that." When she lifted her head, though, she was smiling. "Nothing like a reputation to make the neighbors steer clear of you, is there?"

"If that's your goal, then life is good."

She smiled wider, but it faded quickly. "I'm sorry you got dragged into this."

"I'm not." At all. The weight of the truth scared him senseless.

"Lucas, don't." Pacing to the window, Kristin stared across the street at her house. "I can't do this with you. But... I'm willing to admit there might be something to my brother being involved."

Lucas didn't know whether to cheer or punch a new hole in the wall. She'd thrown cold water on the feelings building for her, but she was willing to admit the truth. He kept his mouth shut, waiting to see what she'd say next.

"I want to believe my brother was a hero."

"He served his country."

She sniffed and tilted her head toward the ceiling. "Serving might be the one good thing he ever did, and even those motives are questionable."

True, and Lucas was glad he hadn't had to be the one to point it out.

"He's somehow tied to everything going on, even though he's gone." Kristin ran a finger along the edge of the window, then flattened her palm against the glass. "This guy keeps mentioning Kyle. I know my brother was far from perfect, but…" Her hand and her head dropped.

Lucas balled his fists and ground them into his thighs. Man, did he ever want to cross the room and hug her, to share the burden, even though she insisted she was fine. Nobody was strong enough to stand alone under an assault like this. She needed somebody.

And Lucas wanted it to be him.

When she didn't say anything else, he gave up all of the fight left in him. He couldn't sit half a room away and watch her battle pain alone. Pushing off the table, he slipped behind her and touched her shoulder.

Kristin flinched, then relaxed and turned, leaning her head against his chest.

At first, Lucas didn't move, scared she'd run like a startled stray cat. Slowly, he wrapped his arms around her and held her close, her tension gradually melting away. Somehow, her leaning on him in spite of all that had already passed between them made Lucas strong again, like he could take on anything thrown their way.

Far from the raging, heart-hammering hurricane that had engulfed Kristin when Lucas kissed her, this embrace brought a whole new kind of peace. In her whole life, even after it became clear her father couldn't reach her anymore, she had never felt this safe, this protected. Until this moment, she hadn't realized how often she'd looked over her shoulder, trying to handle everything in her own power. "What makes you so strong?"

"What?" His voice rumbled, the edges choked.

"Nothing." Kristin pressed her hands against his chest, pushing him away, and he released her without a fight. Right now was not the time, when she was already emotional and at the edge of herself. Tangling her feelings for Lucas with the fear and uncertainty of the threat against her was dangerous, even more dangerous than what her mother had done by letting her emotions rule her heart. She leaned over and snagged a wad of stuffing from a couch cushion and smashed it into her palm. "I'll help you finish cleaning this—"

"No."

The command in Lucas's voice was one she'd never heard before, and it stopped her still. "I'm sorry?" Her voice edged up. He wasn't about to order her around.

"You asked what makes me so strong. I should be allowed to answer." He turned toward her, his face a mask.

She didn't want the answer. Hadn't meant to ask the question in the first place. The last thing Kristin needed was to poke deeper into Lucas Murphy's psyche. "Forget I—"

"No." He leaned against the wall between the window and the front door and crossed his arms, his biceps straining against his shirtsleeves. "You think I'm strong? I'm not."

He was lying. Through everything, Kristin had watched him. He'd never once been shaken, not by anything done to her and not by anything she'd fired to wound him herself. "Nothing rattles you."

The laugh he barked was sharp, and he turned his face toward the ceiling, shaking his head. "Then I put up a good front." He dropped his gaze and captured hers. "You're probably physically and emotionally stronger than I am, but there's one big difference between us."

Her eyes narrowed, but she didn't dignify the comment with a question. It felt like he was baiting her, complimenting her now so he could dig a knife into her back when she let her guard slip. It seemed impossible he could make her feel safe one minute and vulnerable the next, like he was digging into the deepest parts of her soul.

"You can't do this on your own. Nobody can. You know most of my story, but what I didn't tell you— what I should have told you—was there was this chaplain when I was in basic who took an interest in me. Showed me where I was going all out for love in every place but the right one. A lot of people were hurt because of me." He shook his head. "I know it sounds like some cliché that needs to be retired, but the only way you're ever going to be able to truly stand up to what this world throws at you is by giving up."

The words bristled across her skin. Kristin didn't surrender, not to any man and not to a God Who'd let her father destroy their family. She didn't need that kind of brutality. But at the same time, something in Lucas's words wrapped around the broken little girl in her heart and pulled the pieces closer together. The warmth was entirely unfamiliar. Uncomfortable. Almost painful, like a deep-tissue massage after a hard workout, surpassing pain to something wholly right.

She shook her hands out to the side, trying to fling the sensation away. No. No surrender. If there was ever a time when she needed control it was now, when everything indicated her brother had lied to her, when her home and Lucas's had been invaded, when someone was bent on beating nonexistent information out of her. Surrendering was the last thing she'd do.

"Stop talking." Grabbing a couch cushion, Kristin tossed it onto the sofa, straining to make the feelings go away. "This can wait. It's Kyle who can't. We have to focus on him, on who's doing this, not on your…" She waved a hand in the air, then dropped onto the couch cushion she'd set into place. "Not on your happily-ever-after fairy tale."

Lucas opened his mouth then closed it without saying a word. He stared at her for a long time, then turned to the window, letting the silence stretch so long it almost snapped in two. Finally, he stood straighter, but when he spoke, he addressed the window. "What do you want to do?"

"I want to find out what's going on, to prove I'm not involved and to hope Kyle wasn't, either. But if he was…" It hurt to even think it. Yes, he'd had a less-than-stellar reputation even before he joined the army, but a reputation didn't make him an international smuggler. Stuff like that happened in movies, not real life.

Still, like it or not, they had to investigate everything, every angle, if they wanted to stop the madness before it broke her. "If my brother really was involved, then some of his friends were, too, which means somebody at your unit, maybe even Specialist Lacey, is in on this. But how do we figure out who?" There. She'd said it out loud. Practically admitted the unthinkable.

And it hadn't killed her.

Lucas turned away from the window. "The guy who attacked you—would you recognize his voice if you heard it? Did you hear him say enough to pick him out if you heard him speak again?"

Kristin's nose wrinkled. Things had happened so fast and the man had said so few words, his voice low and threatening, likely not the way he'd speak in normal conversation. But she'd seen his stature, broad and muscular, and she'd never forget the eyes of a man who'd been intent on hurting her. She wrapped her arms around her middle, trying not to fly apart, trying not to imagine what might have happened if Lucas hadn't intervened. "I don't know. Maybe. Why?"

"Tomorrow, the battalion is having a mandatory fun day to raise money for the Family Readiness Group. Most of them are family members and volunteers who keep the families informed and plan fun stuff for us to do. It's a crazy job when we're deployed."

"Wait. A mandatory fun day?" Kristin slid to the edge of the couch, a sheen of amusement layering over her confusion and fear. "The army can order you to have fun?"

Lucas grinned. "In a manner of speaking, yes."

"Well, isn't that interesting?" Kristin sat back and tried to get comfortable on the half-stuffed cushion. This turn in the conversation was a whole lot easier than talk of God and smuggling. "Tell me all about this 'have fun or do push-ups' mentality."

"It's not quite that bad. It's basically a workday where you don't work. They're having a cookout and an auction for some things the community donated and…" His grin widened. "And some of the chain of command are putting themselves on the auction block."

"To mow people's yards? Can I bid?"

"Mowing lawns would be less humiliating."

"I'm intrigued." After the tension of the past few days, the light banter felt good…real…easy. Boy, how she could use something easy.

"A cream pie to the face in front of the battalion. Highest bidder gets to pitch the pie." His eyes sparked, like he was ready for whatever bid he got.

"Nice. If you're involved, can I bid?" Shoving a pie into Lucas's face would be fun. Except…the way he'd looked at her yesterday… Something about the idea of him vulnerable, even in fun, undid her. Let her know if she was the one smashing the pie, she'd want to be the one tasting it on his lips, too. Her cheeks warmed, and she leaned over to pick imaginary lint off the carpet at her feet. Anything to keep him from seeing he'd overtaken her thoughts.

He seemed oblivious. "Nope. The guys in the battalion get to bid. I'm guessing I'll go for a pretty low price. It's the officers who will get the heavy bids." He grew serious again. "But there's plenty of social time while we're eating and messing around. Time enough for you to listen and look and see if anybody tweaks your alarms. You in? Even if it creates the impression among the men that you're my date?" The last question came out with a hint of uncertainty Lucas didn't often show.

Kristin ignored it. She could handle idle gossip if it meant proving her brother was innocent. "I'm in." But that was the whole problem. When it came to Lucas, she might not just be in—she might be in too deep.

FOURTEEN

The air between two hulking brick buildings at Lucas's battalion on Fort Bragg hummed with scattered conversations and the sounds of children at play. The March day was perfect, with temperatures in the seventies and sunshine brightening the world. Soldiers gathered in clumps, most holding canned soft drinks while waiting for food to be served. Wives and girlfriends huddled around tables chatting, while smaller groups set out food and coordinated the activities. Across the quad, a group of the ranking soldiers had commandeered the large grill, where smoke wafted across the area and carried the scent of searing burgers and browning hot dogs.

Kristin's stomach rumbled. She didn't usually dive into a hot dog, but the combination of crisp air and sunshine made it sound like the most amazing delicacy in the world. She sipped a bottle of water and tried to tune in to the conversation at the long white plastic table where Lucas had left her in the care of a few spouses and girlfriends. For a while, they'd skimmed conversations about the weather, the news of the week and the latest restaurants coming to Fayetteville, but then

the talk turned to other military bases and new assign-
ments, and her attention had wandered.

To Lucas.

He'd joined the group at the grill about fifty feet
away, but he might as well have settled himself in the
chair right beside her. His eyes were shielded by black
sunglasses, his hair tousled by the breeze, and there was
something about watching him in his element, with the
men he'd fought beside, that squiggled in her stomach
with the kind of hunger a bag of chips and a hamburger
weren't going to satisfy.

A shoulder bumped hers, and one of the women—
Rebecca, maybe?—leaned in closer, an inviting smile
on her face. "So, how did you talk our reclusive Sergeant Murphy into bringing you with him today?"

"What?" Kristin drew her attention from Lucas,
her cheeks warming. How had she let somebody catch
her staring? This was stupid. She was supposed to be
listening for the man who'd attacked her, for anyone
avoiding her or studying her, not surreptitiously watching Lucas. If he was looking her way, it was to see
who was reacting to her presence, not for any other
reason at all.

"Murphy's our quiet man." Rebecca sipped her soda
and settled the can gently on the table. "My husband,
the guy next to him in the Packers shirt, has been trying to get Lucas to meet somebody since the day he
processed into the battalion. Lucas has never taken the
chance. He's the quiet, private type. Keeps to himself.
Friendly and all, but happy as a loner. And now, here
you are." She grinned. "I like you."

"Me? Why?" Rebecca was one of those women who
made everybody welcome, who knew how to have a

conversation with anyone and who seemed as sweet and perfect as her blond hair and blue eyes implied. Kristin had always wanted to be gentle and able to draw people in, but she'd never quite achieved it. She was too competitive and too private to be the type of butterfly Rebecca appeared to be.

"Why wouldn't I like you? Fact is, you probably give Lucas a run for his money, push him to get out more. And you seem like the kind of woman who doesn't take garbage off anybody." Rebecca smiled again. "You'll make an awesome army wife."

Wait. No. Lucas had warned her there'd be talk, and Kristin had been dead certain she could handle it, but marrying her off in the first twenty minutes of the event? If she knew how to get there, she'd walk home before more talk started. "Lucas and I aren't... An army wife? No." Kristin waved her hands like a referee waving off a touchdown. "It's not like that. We're friends. We run together sometimes, but it's not—"

"Okay. You keep right on protesting, and I'll keep right on not believing you." A call from across the quad caught Rebecca's attention. "Oops. I have to go and handle something. But don't fool yourself. You and Murphy are definitely not just friends. It's written all over both of you. Might as well buy T-shirts and proclaim it to the world." She was gone, hustling toward a food table before Kristin could protest further.

Her shoulders slumped. Great. Half the people here would probably have her in a wedding dress by the time dessert was finished. She ought to rethink throwing a pie in Lucas's face. He probably deserved it. Somehow. For something. Even if the speculation wasn't his fault.

For the first time in a long time, Kristin wished she

could be invisible. It seemed as though everyone was staring at her, linking her to Lucas, making them the hot topic of conversation among the groups gathered around the large quad. If she lifted her head at the right time, every eye would probably be on her. Inside, Kristin knew the thoughts were paranoid, but after the past few days, paranoia had almost become her middle name.

Someone slipped into the chair Rebecca had vacated, and Kristin braced herself for more questions and matchmaking before she lifted her head. The new person wasn't another spouse. It was Specialist Brandon Lacey.

She swallowed hard and looked up to see Lucas watching intently. With Kyle mailing a package to Lacey specifically, he was their prime suspect, and now here he was, bold as all get-out, grinning his youthful grin at her. The only thought in her head was Lucas's voice, insisting she didn't know what Lacey was capable of on the battlefield.

"Kristin? Never expected to see you here." He scrubbed his hand across his close-cropped red hair, and his grin widened. "Thanks again for bringing my mail all the way out here."

Now was not the time to get lost in her head, wondering what kind of sociopath Brandon Lacey might be, to be so friendly in front of her and, possibly, so devious behind her back. Now was the time to dig, to see if she could somehow trap him into confessing everything.

If only this would all go down easily. She wanted her life back. And she wanted distance from Lucas. But, really...she didn't.

Kristin shoved away thoughts of Lucas and focused on the young man beside her who could be nothing he seemed, the one link she had to finding the truth, even if the link was rusted and crumbling. "How did your mom like her gift?"

"She won't be here until this weekend. But if you'll give me a phone number, I can let you know."

Kristin fought to keep her mouth closed. This kid was either in on everything and really, really bold, or he'd let loose with the most misguided pickup line she'd ever heard.

Maybe having everybody think she was with Lucas wasn't such a bad thing.

Fighting off a shudder, Kristin tried to pull her spinning thoughts together. She wasn't here to fend off the advances of a kid who might be a killer. She wasn't here to worry about whether or not people thought she was dating, engaged to or even secretly married to Lucas Murphy. She was here to find the man who'd attacked her so she could prove to Lucas he was wrong and her brother was innocent.

Which meant looking Lacey in the eye. Man, did she hate to give him hope. He was a kid. Hopefully an innocent one. Deep in her heart, she was pulling for him to be a bystander.

Kristin inspected him, trying hard to keep her body language disinterested. He was too scrawny to be the man she'd twice encountered, but he could have been padded for some reason. When she caught his eye, she had no doubt he wasn't her attacker. Brandon Lacey's eyes were wide and green, not the narrow darkness of the man intent on harming her. She swallowed her relief, the big sister in her rooting for his innocence. "You have my email. It's not a big deal."

"Yeah, sure." Lacey eased away slightly, his face

falling before he could catch the emotion and turn it around. "I've got some buddies…over there. I've been learning to play old '80s rock on the violin and told them I'd bring it out today." He jerked a vague thumb over his shoulder. "Thanks again. See you around." He wandered over to a group of young soldiers standing near the entrance to one of the buildings.

A group trying not to seem like they were watching. Kristin studied each of them, but the way they milled around, it was hard to tell if they were busy watching her or if they were gawkers at a train wreck, interested in seeing if their buddy crashed and burned.

She turned toward where she'd last seen Lucas, but a line had formed at the grill and he'd vanished. When she angled to check behind her, he was sliding into the seat next to hers, slipping a plate of food in front of her.

"Got you plain chips and a hot dog fully loaded with everything on the table."

Kristin arched an eyebrow. How did he know what she'd been craving?

"You told me one time how cookouts make you think of football, which makes you think of hot dogs, but you hate hot dogs unless they're so crammed with chili and mustard you can't taste the meat." He winked. "That was you, right?"

"It was. Yeah. Thanks." She pulled the plate closer and stared at it, wonder coursing through her. He'd remembered something she'd said ages ago? Something she didn't even remember telling him? That was…

Everything.

Eating what had become a gift from his heart felt a little bit sacrilegious.

"Hey, was I wrong? I can grab you a burger instead if you don't want—"

"No. Really. This is…perfect." And she would not cry over a hot dog.

Kristin leaned back in the metal chair and stared at the white paper plate as she shoved it away. "That did not happen."

Lucas had to laugh. She'd put away as much food as he had, packing in two hot dogs and two snack bags of chips.

Oh, and a plate of banana pudding.

"I'm going to have to run a whole marathon tomorrow to undo this."

Lucas laughed and swallowed a cookie, the very last thing he'd eat today. Well, maybe not the very last. Carpenter's wife had brought an apple pie, and the whole platoon knew how Lucas felt about apple pie. During the deployment, one of the cooks got wind of Lucas's love of the dessert and made one for his birthday. Lucas had polished off the whole thing.

One of the guys was likely to bring him a slice before this day was over. He ought to think twice before eating it, but Kristin? She had nothing to worry about. She was perfect, and a little bit of indulgence wouldn't make a bit of difference. "One day won't hurt you. We've got a long run tomorrow anyway. You'll be fine."

A long run Lucas looked forward to. In spite of everything, including her rebuttal, he was going on with business as usual between the two of them. Something about their routine was comforting, stable. With everything else going nuts, he needed to do something normal, even if sitting beside her and watching her talk with his buddies and hold her own with the other women was definitely not normal.

Even though the more time he spent with her, the more he wanted this to be his new normal.

Man, he needed space. Fast. Kristin James was getting to him more every second. If he stayed this close, he'd either kiss her or spill the feelings he was trying his level best to ignore. She needed time to heal, and he couldn't rush that, not without hurting her worse.

He grabbed her paper plates and stacked them on top of his. "Want more? Auction's gonna start in a little while. You're going to want a good seat, because those pies are all piled with whipped cream."

"No more. Please. I need to sit for a minute and hope I don't pop like a balloon."

His lip curled as he threw his leg over his chair and backed away. "There's a terrible picture."

Her laugh followed him away from the table, layering even more desire into him. Forcing himself to focus on the reasons she was here, Lucas dumped the plates into a large black trash bag and scanned the group. So far, none of the hundred-plus men milling around the area had approached Kristin except for Lacey, and he'd seemed more like a smitten puppy dog than a threat.

Looks could be deceiving, though. Right now Specialist Lacey was on the other side of the quad sawing away on his violin in front of a crowd of soldiers.

Lucas grinned. Half the barracks loved the guy for attempting the opening of an old '80s rock song on that instrument. The other half had threatened the specialist's life on more than one occasion. Today, it appeared he'd found a somewhat appreciative audience for a talent that was probably one of a kind.

Pulling his attention from the small group, Lucas scanned the crowd. No one else seemed to be paying any undue attention to Kristin. Once the wives and girl-friends had finished oohing and aahing over the fact Sergeant Murphy had brought a woman to the battalion, nothing else had happened. Other than Lucas getting to see Kristin in a whole new light, this day was working out to be futile.

He refilled his tea and took the long way to the table, stopping to speak to a few soldiers and to listen in on some conversations. Nothing tickled his gut, which was probably busy with the huge lunch he'd packed in.

At the table, Kristin was leaning forward, talking to Chaplain Freemont a couple of seats away. "How do you handle something like that?"

Apparently, the talk had turned serious. Lucas slipped into his seat and tried not to break the flow of whatever held Kristin's attention.

"Different soldiers handle it different ways. There's a lot of pain when you lose somebody like that."

The words seemed to draw her in. Maybe she'd listen to the chaplain, not shut him out the way she'd slammed the door in Lucas's face when he'd mentioned Jesus yesterday.

The chaplain turned to Rebecca, who was sitting beside Kristin. "I know your husband was there when it happened."

Rebecca stared at something over Lucas's shoulder.

He turned. Hoyt Alston, Rebecca's husband, was mixed in with a group playing football at the open end of the quad. Yeah, it would do Kristin good to hear this story.

"He was. The incident messed with his head the rest

of the deployment." Rebecca turned to the chaplain. "Seeing his buddy there one minute and gone the next when he stepped on an improvised explosive device… Hoyt used to call me, talking about why it wasn't him when he'd been next in line. How he thought he was supposed to be dead because Trewell had kids and we didn't. Nothing I could say got through to him. When he crashed to the bottom, I was pretty sure, one way or another, my husband was coming home in a flag-draped coffin." She lifted her head, face resolute, and nodded toward Chaplain Freemont. "I'm glad you were there."

Lucas knew this story. Kristin needed more than freedom from whoever was coming at her now.

"So am I, but I'm not taking credit." The chaplain leaned back and addressed Kristin, probably the one person at the table who hadn't heard the story. "I'd gone to one of the combat outposts to do a service for the guys, and when I got back, I couldn't find my watch. It was on a clip on my belt. Oldest daughter sent it to me right after we went over."

Somebody on the other side of the table chuckled. Yeah, all the deployed parents were the same way. The little stuff their children sent was more precious than their paychecks. It made Lucas's heart ache for the child he used to be and the kids he'd thought he never wanted to have.

He refused to glance at Kristin, even though he wanted to. Badly.

"I retraced my steps, because I remembered having it in the Humvee, and went back to the motor pool. Sure enough, it was on the ground by the truck. Figured I'd grab it and head to my rack, but when I bent down, I got a good view of the far corner. There was Sergeant

Alston, sitting where nobody could see him except from the angle I was at. We started talking, and before long, it all came out." He nodded at Rebecca.

She sat with a half smile on her face.

Aware of what was coming next, Lucas knew that smile could only come from God.

"What happened?" Kristin was all in, practically falling out of her seat, watching both the chaplain across from her and Rebecca beside her.

"He was planning to end it." Rebecca lifted her chin, her focus on Kristin. "He'd seen Trewell die, had a couple of close buddies killed, had witnessed a lot of other things he'll probably never tell me. He was done. It was all bigger than him. Bigger than us. And along came Chaplain—"

"Jesus." Chaplain Freemont cut her off. "Not me."

"Jesus using the chaplain." Rebecca tossed him a wink. "Hoyt realized he couldn't carry this on his own, and God really did care enough to keep him alive."

"And he felt better." Kristin sat back and crossed her arms, the skepticism on her face grinding Lucas's teeth together.

Rebecca laughed. "Not instantly. It took time. Counseling. Prayer. But Hoyt and I both realized some things are too big for our shoulders. I think that's the night both of us realized Jesus is real. Even when things happen we don't understand, things that hurt worse than physical pain. And reasons are there, even if we never know them." Rebecca realized half of the group around the table was watching her, and she threw her hands in the air, her cheeks pinking. "But this is not about me." She stood. "We've got a football game to break up and an auction to start."

A few of the women followed as the chaplain turned to the soldier next to him and joined a conversation about the upcoming NHL play-offs.

Kristin sat, staring at something in the distance.

In all of his life, Lucas had never felt so helpless. There was nothing he could do to work in her heart. It wasn't up to him, even though he wanted to whisper in her ear how the chaplain was right, Rebecca was right... God loved Kristin and wanted to help her through everything in her life.

But something stopped him. It wasn't his place. It was God's. And he had to trust like never before that this would all end well.

FIFTEEN

Something was stirring and, thankfully, it wasn't the food. This was something deeper. A peace, an ease that overrode her past and even her present precarious circumstances.

This was something she'd never felt before. A call to let go and lay everything down and trust the kind of God Who could send a man a chaplain when he needed him most. The kind of God Who could create a man like Lucas. The kind of God Who could heal pain so violent it overtook entire lives.

Letting go? Yesterday, it had been the worst thing she could imagine. Today? It was attractive as all get-out... and more terrifying than ever.

Kristin's heart pounded so hard, her consciousness rode the edge of darkness. She slid back and almost toppled her chair, catching herself on the edge of the table before she could hit the ground.

Lucas reached for her, his expression dark with concern. "You okay?"

"Yeah. I—" She stood, and her eyes darted around, searching for something to focus on, mind on the verge of panic. Exhaling slowly, she forced herself to center on a trick she'd learned once, grounding herself in her five senses. The sound of children laughing. The smell of smoke from the grill. The warmth of the sun on her skin. The lingering taste of banana from that amazing pudding. The sight of the blue sky overhead.

Nothing threatened her in this moment.

"Tell me how to get to the bathroom?" She needed space to hear her own mind over the pounding of her heart. Hopefully, nobody would stand between her and solitude.

"It's complicated. I can walk with you. You being out of sight for too long isn't the greatest idea, anyway."

"Really?" She rolled her eyes and tried to fake the fight he'd be expecting. "It's the bathroom, not a war zone. I'll be fine."

He eyed her, the challenge in his gaze almost audible, but then his shoulders relaxed and he aimed a finger at the nearest building. "Go in those doors and through the conference room. Hang a right and take the second left and it's about halfway down the hall on your left. Are you sure—"

"I'm sure." She forced another smile she hoped came off as genuine and beat it for the doors.

Inside the building it was dark and quiet. Kristin leaned against the wall in the conference room and waited for her heart to slow its rhythm. The building smelled musty, like no one ever opened the windows and let the air in.

She let her vision adjust to the dimly lit interior, trying to catch a thought. What kind of God let her father kill her mother in front of her before turning the knife on himself? And how could that God be the same God

Who cared enough to make a chaplain lose his watch so a man could be saved?

Her head dropped against the wall with a dull thud. It made no sense. None of it made any sense. How did God decide who lived and who died?

The thoughts unsettled her, made her question the semicomfortable existence she'd built for herself. Questions meant trouble, and she'd had enough trouble to last her seven lifetimes.

Kristin straightened, tugging the hem of her T-shirt straight and squaring her shoulders. The discomfort in her stomach was a by-product of the uncertainty she faced and of trying to prove Kyle's innocence. Nothing more.

She dragged her hands down her face, pulling her cheeks low, surprised to slip through the dampness of tears. Like the child she'd never been, she suddenly longed to go home, missed her mother in a way that pulsed beneath her skin. Her father had robbed her of conversations over coffee, hugs after broken hearts and a listening ear. And the God Rebecca, the chaplain and Lucas trusted allowed it all to happen.

So, no. Surrender wasn't what she needed. Lucas's God wasn't what she needed. What she needed was a splash of cold water on her face before she steeled herself to face the rest of this day. She needed to give a wide berth to the chaplain and Rebecca and anyone else who might raise questions she didn't want to answer... or even to ask in the first place. If she'd driven here herself, then she could beg off and leave without having to wait for Lucas to finish having his mandatory fun.

The oxymoron caught her broadside and made her snicker, easing some of the tension coiled inside. Only the army could invent such a thing, although the men outside seemed to be enjoying the day in spite of the forced festivities.

Her shoes were silent on the tile floors in the still building, and she took the indicated right, finding herself in a long hallway. Now for the second left. This deep in the building, with the office doors closed and the men all outside, the light was milky on the tile floor. Kristin headed the direction Lucas had instructed, but the darkness of the hall and the silence of the building made the hair on the back of her neck stand up. The atmosphere made it feel like dozens of eyes peeked out of darkened doorways, watching her every move. Maybe having Lucas along wouldn't have been such a bad idea after all.

She chuckled at herself. Paranoia. Nothing more. She'd been bruised and battered so many times, it was becoming natural to believe someone was stalking her. Her smile flipped into a frown. Fear like that could never become her norm. Not ever again.

Footsteps, heavy and quick, sounded from a side hallway.

Kristin stopped, her muscles tensing for fight before she could let reason take over. It could be anyone, but with the way things had gone lately, she'd rather not take her chances. She turned to go through the maze of hallways that led outside, but a man appeared at the opposite end of the long passage, his face shadowed. The instant he caught sight of her, he broke into a run.

This was no friend. Adrenaline smacked Kristin in the chest, and she bolted without thinking, her body too bruised to consider a head-on challenge. Pushing deeper into the building that felt like a maze, she took the second left and started trying doors. All locked.

When she reached the bathroom, she hesitated. Hide inside and risk cornering herself, or keep running and hope she found a way out before he found her? She ducked into the bright tile room before he rounded the corner. If nothing else, she could take a position that would allow her to slow him enough to escape.

Ducking into a stall, Kristin pulled out her phone and texted Lucas. 911. She slipped the phone into her pocket, heart pounding so hard she wasn't sure she'd be able to hear the man's approach over it. The normal assurance she could fight off this guy by herself was gone. She'd been beaten, her body and her spirit wounded, and if he was armed... *Please, God, if You're really there, make Lucas hurry.*

For an instant, the stupidity and arrogance of her plan came into focus. It might have been wiser to confront the guy outright in the hallway, to keep running through the building rather than duck into an isolated bathroom with the hopes she could take him out from a fortified position. But running would have kept her from texting Lucas for help. She had to make her stand and fight.

The dull thud of footsteps drew closer, heavy and slow, like he was expecting the ambush she'd hastily planned.

The exterior door scraped lightly across the floor as it opened, the footsteps heavier than ever. Kristin knew, with a sudden rush of hot adrenaline, if he'd truly followed her in here, this was serious. There was no choice now but to stand and fight, because there was no way her pursuer's intentions were honorable.

She had a pretty good idea of what he wanted. But she also knew the price he'd pay for trying to get it.

Wishing she had worn her hiking boots instead of light cross-trainers, Kristin held her breath and waited, muscles steeled, until running shoes appeared beneath the stall door. Bracing for leverage, she planted her foot against the door with a kick so hard, the latch snapped off and skittered across the floor. The jolt vibrated through her knee and into her sore hip as the door blasted open, colliding with her assailant and driving him backward with a dull thud.

Kristin didn't wait to see if he recovered. Instead, she scrambled for the door, fingers brushing the handle before the man grabbed her collar, jerking her to him and cutting off her air.

He dragged her closer and held her tight against his chest, leaning toward her, the rough fabric of his ski mask scrubbing her cheek. "Let's talk about Kyle."

She kicked and struggled, but he tightened up on her, his voice deepening. "Don't make me hurt you. Please. Where did Kyle hide everything?"

"What's everything?"

He trapped her against his chest; she couldn't move, couldn't even take a full breath. "You already know. Where is it?"

Shouts echoed from the hallway as pounding feet drew closer.

Kristin almost sagged in relief, but she thought better of it and whipped her head back hard, connecting with her attacker's face.

He howled and dropped her.

She smashed to the floor on one knee as the door flew open and bounced off the opposite wall.

Lucas charged in, wild-eyed, crossing the floor and driving a fist into the man's jaw in one motion.

He staggered but charged into the fight until more men poured into the small space and he stopped, frozen in place, working his jaw back and forth, like it hurt or he was calculating an escape.

Kristin slid to the side and took an offered hand to pull herself to her feet, but she refused to lean on the soldier for support.

Lucas jerked the mask from her attacker's head, his expression stormy as he got a good look at Kristin's attacker. "Specialist Cronin?" His voice deepened as he balled his fists and went chest to chest with the man, the set of his jaw saying he was prepared to tear the guy in two. "You and I have—"

"Murphy." The command came from a man who pushed through the crowd, clearly an authority. "The military police are on the way. Don't get yourself tangled in this any worse than you already are."

Lucas didn't move, just stood toe-to-toe with Cronin, anger radiating off him.

"Lucas." Kristin laid a hand on his shoulder, focusing on his anger easier than dealing with the fear threatening to swamp her. "I'm fine." Her voice betrayed her, breaking the word in two.

He appraised her before he backed off. "Really?"

She nodded, but the intensity with which he studied her almost buckled her knees. Only the audience of the soldiers and families who had come running with Lucas and the chaos of men taking Cronin into custody kept her from reaching for Lucas. Specialist Cronin might be in custody, but he wasn't the man who had come at her in her kitchen. He wasn't the man who had attacked her on the trail. It was clear she wasn't safe at home or in public…anywhere.

She'd run out of places to run.

The rage in Lucas's veins raced fast and hot, but as he locked eyes with Kristin, the emotion pulsing through him was entirely different. When he'd thrown the door open, he'd been sure he could tear the man who'd come after Kristin into tiny pieces and enjoy every moment. But now, the way she was looking at him, like he was some kind of hero…now he wanted to pull her out of the fray and hold her, to reassure himself she was all right and he'd made it to her in time.

He never should have let her come into the building alone. Now one of his own soldiers stood against the wall, guarded by the chain of command. One of his own soldiers. One of the men he'd fought for and beside had attacked Kristin, had likely trashed his house. Would have done who knew what if she hadn't gotten a text off in time.

He had to ease up. Now. Before he embraced Kristin in front of his men and scared her away forever.

Reluctantly, Lucas turned away toward Specialist Cronin as sirens wailed closer, the sight of the man ripping away his concern for Kristin and replacing it with fury.

He edged closer, but before he could say a word, Travis was in front of him, blocking the path. "Luke, back off before you do something stupid. I see it all over your face." Travis's voice was low enough to stay between them. "Let somebody else handle this before you find yourself in cuffs right beside him."

As much as he wanted to shove Travis out of the way

and put a fist through Cronin's face, he let the words sink in. Kristin was safe. And hopefully, finally, this was all over. She'd be safe.

He fired a hard look over Travis's shoulder at Cronin, who seemed more like a scared kid than a ruthless killer. He stared at the floor, blood streaking from his nose, shaking... Either he was a really good actor or being faced down by a crew of angry soldiers in a women's restroom was his undoing.

The commander pushed his way to the middle of the room and addressed the soldiers trying to crowd the small bathroom. "Clear out. Now. Go home, go to the barracks, but don't stay here. Let the MPs do their job."

The silent mob cleared the room, obeying orders, even though they'd likely hang out in the hall or the parking lot to gawk. Nobody was getting a pie in the face today after all.

Lucas reached for Kristin and wrapped an arm around her, easing her out the door as the crowd thinned. His presence kept anyone from rushing her to offer support or ask questions. While she shivered slightly against him, she appeared none the worse for wear. At least it probably seemed so to everyone else. Lucas knew well enough by now the way Kristin could put up an amazing front. Inside, she was rattled. He had no doubt. "Tell me the truth." He stopped walking and turned her toward him, planting his hands on her shoulders so he could look at her. "Are you really okay?"

Kristin shrugged away, watching something over his shoulder. "I said I'm good."

She wasn't, but now wasn't the time to press her, not with an audience milling around. "Paramedics may want to give you a once-over."

"Why? I'm fine. Really. He didn't hurt me." She glanced around then edged him up the hall out of the way. "We've got a problem."

All desire for her vanished at the expression on her face. It wasn't fear—more like dread, like something very, very bad was wrong. Lucas pulled her farther out of hearing of the group slowly filtering out of the building in the opposite direction. "What?"

"Your soldier..."

"Specialist Cronin."

"Cronin. He's not the guy who's been coming after me. Both of them were intent on hurting me, on intimidating me. Cronin, he..." She shook her head, confusion marking her features. "Lucas, he went out of his way not to hurt me, almost pleaded with me instead of bullying me. Not like the other times."

"He cornered you in a bathroom, put his hands on you..." The echo of Lucas's voice bounced off the wall. "He sure wasn't trying to talk to you about the weather."

She laid a hand on his arm and gave him the same kind of silent threat his aunt used to give him when she wanted him to lower his voice. "I'm not saying he's innocent, just that he's not the same guy."

"You're dead certain?"

"It's like I told the police the other day. The guy on the trail—"

A military police officer appeared at her elbow. "Miss James? We need to speak to you."

Her spine stiffened, and she glared at the wall with a hard resolve. This had to be hard for her, these constant reminders of the night her mother had been killed.

Travis leaned against the wall beside Lucas and held out a water bottle. "She's holding up better than you are. Kristin's a tough one. Paramedics said she broke Cronin's nose."

Of course she did. Kristin had told him more than enough times she could take care of herself, and she insisted on proving it over and over. Still, the constant attacks had begun to wear on her. The facade was cracking.

Lucas studied Kristin's face as she talked to the officer, the impassive expression she wore saying this was an ordinary conversation and not an official statement to the police after another attempt on her life. How did she get to be so ice-cold? She'd really driven her emotions deep if she could come out of this as unfazed as she appeared to be. Then again, this was Kristin James. Appearances could be deceiving. Lucas knew she was roiling inside over yet another conversation with the police, yet another reminder of the night her father violently ripped her life apart.

"So, I was noticing something you might want to check into."

Lucas turned from Kristin to Travis, who seemed to be chewing on something pretty serious. "What's that?"

"Naturally, most of the wives packed and left and most of the married soldiers went with them. But the whole platoon's out on the quad milling around."

"So? It's like a train wreck. They want to see what happens next."

"Right." Travis chuckled. "More like they want another chance to ogle the hot chick who defended herself against a trained soldier. Your girlfriend's going to be legendary."

"Not my girlfriend."

"I know. And you can say it all you want, but they're

going to keep thinking it. Your street cred's headed through the roof, Murph."

Enough. "Is that what you came in here to tell me?"

"No." Travis grew serious again. "All of your guys are out there except Cronin, naturally. And Lacey."

Lucas's muscles froze. All this chaos was roaring and Lacey, the one who'd shown the most interest in Kristin, the one who'd received a package from her brother, was the one missing? "You're sure?"

"Dead certain. I poked around. Nobody's seen him since right after lunch, when he was sawing away on that violin. Last I heard, he broke a string and headed to his room to grab another. Do you think—"

"Do I think he's in on this?" Most definitely. If Lacey had disappeared shortly before Kristin was attacked, then he could be anywhere by now. On the run, watching Kristin...

Her voice drifted to him. "I'm certain this is a different man. The other man had a tattoo on his leg. Specialist Cronin's wearing shorts, and there's no snake crawling up his shin."

Lucas straightened, forgetting Travis's words as his face slackened. He hadn't heard right. It was impossible. He should have listened to her statement at the lake, should have asked for every detail sooner. This would have ended before she ever got hurt the second time. He'd blown it.

Kristin was still describing the tattoo, but Lucas already saw it in his mind. "It wrapped around his shin. The fangs were bloody and aimed at his knee."

Lucas's jaw clenched so tight, he had to strain to speak. "I know who's after her." The only person Lucas knew who had a tattoo like that was in the wind somewhere, cut loose from the unit last week after a positive drug test overseas. It all made sense. Specialist William Morrissey had been friends with Kyle Coleman and Brandon Lacey overseas, a good soldier until Coleman was killed. Then the problems started. After the drug test, he'd redeployed with the unit and been confined to quarters until he chaptered out of the army last week.

Just in time to start harassing Kristin.

"What did you say?" Travis straightened as well.

"I know who's doing this, and if I'm right, Lacey's probably involved."

Lucas straightened and glanced at the MP questioning Kristin. She'd be safer with him than she'd be if he spouted off his suspicions. He marched for his office, where he snatched the keys to the barracks rooms. If Lacey was hiding himself or anything else upstairs, his time was running out. "Go outside and tell the MPs William Morrissey is the ringleader."

"Morrissey?" Travis's face mirrored Lucas's emotions.

"The tattoo. Morrissey got that snake after he took shrapnel to the knee two years ago."

Travis blocked the door. "Let the cops handle this, Luke. Don't go rogue now, not this close to the end."

"No." Lucas went toe-to-toe with his friend, all of his frustration unleashing in one direction. The wrong one, sure, but he was a volcano with nowhere else to blow. Nobody, not even Travis, was keeping him from putting a stop to what was happening to Kristin. If he didn't move now, Lacey could vanish along with Morrissey, and no one would ever find them. "You go tell the MPs and they'll be upstairs right behind me. But I want to see him face-to-face before he has a chance to put on his game face for the cops. I want to surprise him with the question about Morrissey's involvement."

He shoved Travis aside, hating to leave Kristin behind but unwilling to wait any longer to confront Specialist Lacey. Everything was falling into place, and he wasn't letting one detail slip through his fingers.

Travis didn't hesitate any longer, but turned and headed for the building's entrance at full speed to bring the MPs running.

At this point, Lucas was past caring. He wanted Kristin safe. Then she could focus on getting her head on straight with God and then maybe, just maybe, getting her heart straight with him.

On the third floor, Lucas stopped and pounded his balled fist on a heavy wood door. "Lacey, open the door."

Silence.

He pounded the door again, determined to make this the last play of the game. "Last chance, Specialist."

Again, nothing.

Tensed and ready for a confrontation, Lucas slid the key in the lock and threw the door open.

The metallic smell smacked him immediately, familiar and stomach churning. He inhaled sharply, his face tightening, and shoved the door open farther.

Everything in the room was tossed, the destruction complete, the smell of blood overwhelming.

Lucas edged into the room and pulled his T-shirt over his nose, eyes watering, heart pounding with the kind of sick knowing years of battlefield experience brought. He turned to the left and tried not to gag.

In the center of the room, Lacey lay facedown, his head at an odd angle, blood pooled and running from the deep cut in his neck.

SIXTEEN

"At what point did you lose the common sense God gave you, Murphy?" Major Anderson slammed the door to his office and walked around his desk to face Lucas and Travis, who stood like privates called out for mischief in basic training.

Lucas couldn't decide if he was more humiliated by the trouble he was in or disgusted by the image of Lacey's body, head practically severed. If there was a way to turn back time, he would, and he'd have gone with Travis to send the military police to Lacey's room. He definitely wouldn't have gone rogue and dragged Travis with him. "Sir, this is all me. Sergeant Heath was trying to talk me out of—"

"No." Travis stood straighter. "I let him go."

"Well, you're both loyal, even when you're stupid." The major eyed the two of them, then sank into his chair. "Sit. Both of you." He waited for them to obey, then simply sat there, eyeing them with the same fierce expression that made privates curl up like armadillos. "I had to stop the MPs from taking you in, Murphy. You'd better be glad there's accountability for you every single minute of this day until you found Specialist Lacey. If you'd been out of sight at any time, you'd be in custody right now."

It was true. Lucas had found the body, was away from the group. And if Lacey was truly involved, he had a motive.

"If Lacey is a part of this ring CID is investigating, do you realize your presence outside today is the one thing keeping you off the hook for his murder? Especially after the way you went after Cronin this afternoon. You lost your head." The major kneaded his forehead, probably fighting the headache they'd caused. "Women can make the smartest man stupid." He aimed a finger at Travis. "And somehow, it always comes back to you."

Lucas clamped down on his tongue. He was in enough trouble without trying to defend Travis or his own relationship with Kristin. Nobody here would ever again believe they were only friends. Not after today. If he was being honest, even he didn't believe it anymore. "Sir, where is Kristin James right now?" He hadn't seen her in over an hour, not since they'd called the MPs to Lacey's room. The major had ordered them to his office and made them wait while he and the first sergeant ran interference upstairs. The worry in Lucas's gut competed with the seared-in image of Lacey's body to turn his stomach inside out. He had to get to her, to make sure Morrissey didn't do to her what he'd done to Lacey. Lucas had no doubts he was behind the murder and everything else.

"She's fine. Friend of hers, a Staff Sergeant Jordan, took her home."

Casey. At least she was safe. Relatively. As long as

the MPs found Morrissey quickly, Kristin would be fine. If they didn't...

Lucas squashed the thought. Right now, he had to hold himself in neutral if he wanted to get out of here and back to her side, the one place he felt his presence was doing any good.

Major Anderson studied Lucas's reaction, then turned to Travis. "Specialist Lacey is definitely dead, but you probably knew on sight. Somebody was waiting for him. Whoever killed him found some leftover violin string in his room and made themselves a garrote. Lacey didn't have a chance. Severed his neck to the spine. Hard to say, with the weapon being fashioned in his room, if it was related to CID's investigation or if it was a crime of passion. Half the barracks was tired of him sawing on that violin of his."

"A weak motive for murder." Travis wasn't biting on the dark battlefield humor the major threw out as a coping mechanism. "Are they searching for William Morrissey?"

"They are in connection with the attack on Kristin James, but without a motive, they aren't prepared to say he killed our soldier."

Lucas tightened his grip on the arm of the chair. They had to find Morrissey and stop this. "What about the box Kristin delivered to Lacey?"

"In the room. A cheap tea set and some jewelry in it."

So it really was a gift for his mom. Lucas wasn't sure he could handle many more punches to the gut today.

Major Anderson leaned forward. "You know, Murphy, Major Draper is itching for a reason to take you into custody right now. Says you're in deep, too close to Kristin James. Seems like everything that happens to her, there you are. He wants you out of the way, and he'll use any excuse to do it."

They couldn't order him to stay away from her. Not now. He'd never violated a direct command before, but if it meant the difference between Kristin's safety and leaving her to the wolves...

The commander waved off Lucas's coming argument. "Somebody has to keep an eye on her until the authorities locate Morrissey, and I can argue with you all day, but it's going to be you. I'm no fool. But you listen to me." He leaned across the desk, gaze hard on Lucas's. "Let the investigators do their job. You make sure she's safe. But no digging for evidence. No going rogue. And no more running ahead of the authorities like you know more than they do. You hear me?"

"Yes, sir." As far as Lucas was concerned, he was getting off way too easy. Almost made him wonder if there was something going on he didn't know yet.

The commander turned to Travis. "Heath, you keep him in line. Between the two of you, you're the one without a dog in this fight."

"Yes, sir."

"Go home. I'll call you if there's anything you need to know. And for the sake of all of our careers, stay out of trouble." The major stood and waved them toward the door.

Lucas reached for the doorknob, glad to still have his rank, his job and his freedom.

"Murphy."

He stopped and turned, trying not to wince. "Sir?"

"Good to see you found somebody."

Travis choked.

Lucas didn't find it one bit funny. He stormed out

the door and was halfway down the hall before Travis caught him. "So, Luke, did you find somebody?"

"Shut up."

"Sorry. Bad timing." Travis fell into pace with him as they headed for the front doors. "You're not finished with this yet, despite what Major Anderson said, are you?"

Lucas didn't even stop walking. There was no reason to explain himself, not when Travis already knew the truth. Until Lucas knew for sure Morrissey was the bad guy, he wasn't going to stop searching. Kristin needed to be safe. For good. No doubts. He shoved out the front door into the dark evening.

"Not on your life."

Kristin paced from the back door, through the kitchen and into the living room, the hardwood creaking beneath her feet. It had been radio silence since Lucas disappeared three hours ago while she was giving her statement, a man on a mission. His phone went straight to voice mail, and she had no one else to contact concerning him.

Everything had been fine until the MPs bolted into the building, leaving Kristin with one officer until Casey came to bring her home. When the ambulance arrived right before Casey did, no one would say a word about whom it was there for. She'd been blocked from any information, though she'd heard a brief smattering of radio traffic. A brief burst that had included Lucas's name.

She dug her teeth into her lower lip. If anything had happened to Lucas because of her...

"Stop pacing. You'll have to replace the hardwood if you don't." Casey sat in her customary chair, trying to come across as relaxed. Her rigid posture and the tight measure in her voice said she was as worried as Kristin.

Stopping in the middle of the room, Kristin stared at the curtained front window, where the dark of an early-spring Carolina evening peeked black around the edges. She needed something to do. Some distraction to keep her mind off wild imaginings featuring Lucas being loaded into an ambulance and rushed away. Her hands were too shaky to paint the bathroom. Her legs too weak for a workout. And she definitely should have skipped the three cups of coffee she'd tossed back since she got home.

Helpless, she could only stare, keenly aware of her lack of place in Lucas's life, even though he'd over-taken every aspect of her own. "I don't know what to do. There's nobody to tell me if something happened. I'm a friend, nothing else. So how long do we wait before we go to post?"

"If something had happened, Travis would have called."

"He doesn't have my number, not unless Lucas gave it to him."

Casey cleared her throat and shifted in her chair. "He has mine."

Well, there it was. Kristin had asked for a distraction. This one was as good as any.

She pivoted slowly on one heel and faced her friend. "Do tell."

"You know it's no big deal." Casey shrugged off the question in Kristin's voice. "The night we went for pizza, he asked for it. We've talked once since then."

"I see." Kristin sank to the edge of the coffee table, relieved to have something else to talk about. If Travis was into Casey, this might be just what her friend needed to realize she was more amazing than she thought. "The night you went for pizza was last night."

"And we've talked once. Like I said, no big deal. He was probably bored."

"Probably bored? Are you—"

"Let's talk about you instead." Casey leaned over and poked her finger into Kristin's bicep, her smile widening, probably because she was about to go on the offensive. "You've paced this house for almost two hours. And you've dialed Lucas Murphy's phone number how many times now?"

"Because he's my friend and I'm worr—"

"No."

"He's—"

"No. Have you ever paced the floor for two hours over me? I'm your friend, too." Sitting back, Casey flattened her hands on the table, her smile smug. "Something more is going on here. Maybe you should be the one talking, not me."

There wasn't much to tell. He'd kissed her. She'd pushed him away. Things had been slightly off between them ever since, closer yet farther away all at the same time. The one certain thing in her life right now was the way Lucas made her feel safe, and she was terrified that safe place was gone forever.

"I don't know what you're afraid of, Kris. Lucas isn't your dad. He's not your brother, either."

"He scares me."

Casey laughed. "Lucas doesn't scare you. You scare you. You let him in and now you don't know how to kick him out. I'm not even sure you want to."

The thud of footsteps on the porch kept Kristin from

answering. She glanced at Casey, her heart thumping. This was about to be very, very bad or…worse. She was on her feet and at the peephole before anyone could knock, Casey right behind her.

Lucas's face on the other side weakened her muscles in relief, and she pressed her hand against the door to keep her balance. Him safely on her porch was the most amazing sight she'd ever seen.

She pulled the door open and stared at him through the screen, wanting to throw herself at him and confess… What? That she didn't want to contemplate life without him? No. That wouldn't work, especially not with an audience like Casey and Travis. "Why didn't you call?"

The accusation in her tone jerked his chin up. "My phone's on my desk at work. We had to shut them off when…" Their eyes locked through the screen. "Honestly, all I could think about was getting here as fast as I could."

Kristin's stomach dropped in a way she'd never felt before…in a way she hoped to experience again. Maybe. It was almost too good. Problem was, it took her ability to form words with it, and she couldn't stop staring at Lucas, sinking into the implication behind his words.

"Okay, let the men in the house." Casey reached around her and shoved the screen door open. "They didn't come here to stand on the porch all night."

Kristin had almost forgotten anyone else was in the house. She pushed the door open and gave Lucas enough room to come through without touching her. If he did, she'd—

Well, she had no idea what she'd do, but it would definitely be something she could never take back.

"What happened?" She found her voice somewhere

around her feet. "What was with the MPs and the ambulance? We thought…" Never mind what she'd thought. Confession would tip her hand about feelings she wasn't even certain of herself.

"Have you got coffee ready? I could really use lots of strong coffee." Without the screen to mask his features, Kristin got a good look at Lucas's expression for the first time. His face was pale and tight, almost like he'd encountered something he never wanted to see again.

Casey was halfway to the kitchen. "I'm on it."

"Right behind you." Travis was gone, too, leaving Kristin and Lucas alone.

Leaving Kristin free to step into Lucas's embrace and to reassure herself of his safety. But she also wanted answers. With worry wearing off, anger rose. "What happened on post to make you bolt? And what's kept you out of touch? It had to be bad. I can see it all over your face."

Lucas shook his head, then rolled his eyes to the ceiling like he was praying.

"You're scaring me." Something was way wrong. He had the same demeanor about him as the man who'd come to the door to tell her Kyle was gone. That *I want to be anywhere else* stance that spoke of bad news on the way.

Finally, he pointed to the couch. "You might want to sit."

"Really?" She wasn't some weak female who was going to faint at the slightest bad news, even though her legs had nearly given out when she'd spotted Lucas safely outside her door. "You can tell me here and now."

"Brandon Lacey's dead. Murdered."

The stark declaration robbed Kristin's knees of strength.

She sank to the coffee table and stared at Lucas. This wasn't possible. He'd sat beside her a handful of hours ago, his awkward attempt to get her phone number almost endearing. "How?"

"I don't think you—"

"How?"

Lucas settled beside her, barely an inch away. He clasped his hands and pressed his thumbs into his forehead, which was lined with grief and something unreadable but so much worse. "We found him in his room. Someone strangled him with his violin strings."

The same violin he'd been playing '80s rock on? Kristin laughed, the hysterical laugh that meant her mind had been pushed over the edge. A laugh like she hadn't laughed since before the night her father changed everything. But then the laughter turned to gasping and the gasping to tears. Lacey was a kid. No matter what he'd done, he was a kid. And he didn't deserve to die with his head half-severed, in his own room, where he should have been safe.

She choked on a sob. Then Lucas's arms were around her, and he pulled her to his side, planting a kiss on the top of her head, letting her cry until the tears were gone. Nobody had ever done that for her, held her close and shared her grief. She'd always cried alone. When her parents died, when Kyle died… Always alone. This was so much more. So much easier.

When the tears were gone, Kristin didn't pull away, simply sat on her coffee table, her head buried in Lucas's neck, smelling soap and soldier. She was spent. And she didn't care if she never moved again.

But she pulled away, swiping her shirtsleeve across her eyes and straightening her posture. She had to be strong. They had to figure this out. For Kyle and for Lacey. "Now what?"

"Now we wait. CID is searching for the man we think is the ringleader."

Kristin's heart pounded faster. "They know who's behind this?"

"Possibly. A former soldier in the company. A friend of your brother's."

She'd thought she was all out of tears, but her eyes stung with fresh grief. "So it still comes back to Kyle." Kristin stared at the ceiling, fending off the growing suspicion she was wrong about Kyle's guilt and Lucas was right. "I don't know what to do." Since the night her mother died, she'd never felt so helpless.

"We have an idea." Travis led Casey into the room, and the pair handed out mugs of hot coffee.

Kristin set hers to the side. More caffeine would probably kill her.

Casey sat in her usual chair while Travis stood by the front door, facing them. "Casey and I were talking and we're wondering…if Kyle Coleman was involved and his buddies are, too, then where's the stuff? It's like only Kyle knew. Kristin keeps saying these guys all ask where he hid his stash. So that's my question. Where is it?"

Hopelessness settled on Kristin like a rock. She could no longer formulate excuses for Kyle. Right now, she felt like the lone link between her brother and the truth, and she knew less than nothing. "I don't know. Somehow, everybody thinks I know, but Kyle never sent me anything. The only package he ever mailed here was the one for Specialist Lacey."

"Which didn't have anything in it but a glass tea set

and a couple of pieces of cheap jewelry, all of which could be bought at any market over there." Lucas shifted away from her and took a long sip of coffee so hot it had to be scalding. He didn't seem to notice. "If there was something more in there, then whoever killed Lacey took it, if Lacey didn't ditch it sooner."

"So it really was a gift for his mom." She wanted to be sick. How did she end up surrounded by bloodshed?

"I'm sorry. It looks that way." Lucas glanced at her and back down at his coffee. "We have to think about Kyle, though. The other thing to consider is he never sent anything else to you. If he was really smuggling and using you to do it, he would have mailed you dozens of packages."

"Unless…" Kristin stood and walked over to stand beside Travis, her mind spinning in possibilities. "Unless he brought something with him on R & R. He was home for two weeks right before he died. He stayed here while he was home, so it's possible there really is something in my house."

"Okay, then." Lucas set his cup aside and stood. "Somebody needs to search the house and somebody needs to go and watch what's going on at the barracks, maybe try to talk to some of the guys. Flip a coin?"

"Wait a second, Luke." Travis's mouth set into a grim line. "You're putting a lot on the line if you keep digging."

"I know."

"Well, then, as long as you know." Travis's eyes sparked mischief. "Casey and I will take the barracks." He drained his coffee and handed the cup to Kristin before turning to Casey. "If you're up for it."

"I'm game." She was out the door with him before anyone could argue. Again.

"Well, all right." Lucas turned from staring at the closed door after them and looked at Kristin. "It's you and me. Where do we start?"

"In the attic, and we'll work our way down." She turned to the door and punched in the alarm code. The last thing they needed was anyone sneaking up on them while they were upstairs.

She followed Lucas to the stairs. Actually, the way she was starting to lean on him, the last thing she needed was to be alone with Lucas Murphy ever again.

SEVENTEEN

"Nobody's attic should be this clean." Lucas braced his hands in the doorway and leaned into the A-framed space. There wasn't a cobweb to be found. The rafters were dust-free and even the plywood floor was swept. Other than two plastic storage containers, there was nothing to indicate anyone had built a life in the house.

Kristin swept her bangs away from her face, her hair not caught in a headband for once, and surveyed the unfinished room, looking everywhere but at him. "You want it to be dirty?"

"Are you kidding?" He was used to his aunt's attic, filled with the accumulated belongings of his family, packed to the rafters with boxes of his grandparents' things, which she'd inherited after his grandmother died. This? This was not right. "Attics are crowded and dusty and full of stuff. You don't have any, you know, junk?"

"Like what?" She crossed her arms and waited, something between bemusement and hurt tickling her features, like his next answer would determine her mood for the rest of their search.

Which wouldn't last long if the other rooms in her house were as pristine as this attic. It wouldn't surprise him, based on the order in her kitchen. "Stuff. Like, I don't know. Stuff from when you were…" *A kid*. From her family.

Well, he'd messed this one up, and the misstep made his neck burn. It made sense she'd have very little of her past stored away. It made sense she'd *want* very little to remind her. "Never mind." He slapped his hands together and wished for a way to rewind the last ninety seconds. "What's in the two boxes over there?"

She dropped her arms to her sides, and her eyebrow arched. For a second, Lucas thought she was going to pursue his stupidity to its conclusion, but then she exhaled loudly. "Kyle's. He brought them over before he deployed and asked me to store them. I've never gone through them. Actually forgot they were here."

Lucas's heart beat faster. It couldn't be that easy, could it? That they could walk into her attic and find millions in missing antiquities?

There were only two boxes, so whatever was in them would have to be small. Maybe they held some clue, a key, a map…

He'd lost his mind, turning this into a hunt for pirate treasure.

Kristin stood staring at the boxes like they might bite her. She didn't make a move toward them.

This couldn't be easy for her, acknowledging the possibility of her brother's guilt and digging through his things. "You want me to do this?"

She lifted her head, her bottom lip caught between her teeth, then turned toward the boxes. "I just…" She blew the bangs out of her face again. "Regardless of what he did, he was my brother. The only family I had left, the only blood…" She shrugged. "I don't know what I want to be in those boxes."

Lucas reached for her hand and laced his fingers with hers. He knew if he put his arms around her, he might never let go. He'd fallen too far, and she didn't need that kind of attention.

She needed a friend.

"I get it. If it's smuggled goods, then this is over, but your brother was a thief. If it's anything else, then you're still in the crosshairs, and your brother's involvement is still ambiguous."

She nodded with grim resignation, then squeezed his fingers and let go. "Let's do this."

Dropping to her knees in front of a green plastic tub, she popped the lid and removed the contents without any more hesitation. Shirts and blue jeans grew in a small pile around her before she leaned in and looked at the empty container, the brave face he was starting to recognize as a facade set firmly into place. "Clothes."

Lucas knelt beside her and dragged a hand through the second box. More of the same. He emptied the container anyway, tossing a pair of jeans to the side. They landed with a dull thud, heavier than they should have been.

Kristin's head came lifted. "You heard that, too, right?"

Something was stuffed in the two front pockets of the jeans. Lucas reached in and wrapped his fingers around the contents of the first pocket, pulling out what he found.

Money.

Both pockets held two folded bundles of money.

Without exchanging words, the two dived into the

rest of the pants and shirts, searching the pockets until they had several folded stacks of bills. A quick count yielded nearly ten thousand dollars.

Kristin rocked back on her heels and stared at the money in Lucas's hand. "What's this mean?"

"I have no idea. Either he didn't trust the banks with his savings or—"

"I'm not sure if Kyle had any savings. He poured quite a bit of money into the Camaro. At least…that's what he told me."

"And now the car's missing." Frankly, anything Kyle had told his sister meant nothing. He'd have said whatever it took to keep his hide out of trouble. Lucas had witnessed that trait in the specialist firsthand and more than once.

"This is pointless." Kristin dropped and sat on the floor, propping her forearms on her bent knees. "Since he left, I've cleaned my house dozens of times, even under beds and in closets. It's what I do when I can't sleep. I've never seen anything out of the ordinary. Maybe this is all about the money. Maybe what Morrissey and Cronin are after is cash."

"Maybe." Lucas restacked the bills and stared at them. It was possible, but it didn't make sense. If it was all about the money, why steal her keys? Why not break in while she was gone and tear the place apart until they found it? There was no need to physically attack Kristin, to wait until she was home and then come inside.

No, something else was going on. Something he couldn't quite lay a finger on. "Tell me exactly what Cronin said to you."

She closed her eyes. Lucas really didn't know how she could hold out much longer, with her brother's guilt becoming more obvious. "He wanted to know where Kyle hid 'everything,' whatever 'everything' is."

"Money is money or cash. It's not 'everything.' If it was money, he'd have used different terms, right?" Lucas was putting a lot of weight on semantics, but he'd take anything at this point. "Did Kyle have a storage unit?"

"Not that I know of. I closed his checking account. Unless he was paying cash, there was nothing to indicate he had a place. My brother was… I don't know anymore. Maybe I've been in denial, wanting him to be family while he was incapable. Maybe I expected too much." She shifted and leaned against the wall, turned her face to the rafters and shut her eyes, the brown waves of her hair brushing her chin. "All this makes me wonder if you're for real."

It took a second for the words to register. The soft vulnerability she was displaying in the semidarkness was more distracting than it needed to be. Where was she headed? "If I'm for real?"

"I don't understand you. You…" She swept her hand out but didn't open her eyes. "You have to be involved in this, watching your guys—I get that. But I don't understand you being here now, helping me." She lifted her head and caught him looking. "Putting yourself between danger and me. Nobody's ever done that for me before."

Maybe nobody had ever been in love with her before. He dug his fingers into the thin plastic box, the truth catching him hard in the chest. He'd known things were going too far, but now, sitting here with her, he knew how far. He loved her. Loved her quirks and her heart. Loved her strength and the vulnerability she was just beginning to explore.

He was in love with Kristin James.

The words begged to be spoken, but Lucas held them. Something grabbed him by the shoulder and pushed him into place, kept him from moving nearer, from telling her what had been slowly overtaking his life ever since the day she'd edged him out at the finish line of a half marathon. It had never been about training for him, even though he'd tried to tell himself it was.

It had always been about her.

This was so much different than anything he'd felt in the past. Sometime in the past two months, he'd changed. Being around Kristin, putting her before himself…he was capable of the kind of love he'd never imagined he would be. The truth struck like a sucker punch from the left. He opened his mouth to tell her, but the urge to keep quiet overrode everything. It was like something inside said *wait*, and he couldn't defy the order.

Kristin smiled faintly, but it didn't quite reach her eyes. "And then the chaplain, Rebecca, you…you all start talking about Jesus, Who supposedly stands between me and danger all the time. How do you believe in something you've never seen?"

There it was. The reason for the *wait*. Lucas could make this all about him, could tell her he loved her and could protect her. Or he could tell her the bigger truth and release her into the hands of Someone who loved her more than Lucas ever could. It went against every ounce of flesh he had, but he knew what he had to do.

"I guess I've seen enough to know." The words strained. Man, he wanted so badly to touch her right now, to wrap her tight against him and shield her, but that would shift the focus to him. Sitting here in the stillness of her attic, in what was surely the calm before yet another storm, he had to come second.

No, he had to come last.

"It's not anything I've seen from the outside. It's what I've seen in me." When she didn't say anything, just kept staring at him as though she was hooked on his every word, he plunged in, praying his words would have the impact they needed. "I went after love everywhere. I mean it. Nothing ever filled me until that chaplain talked to me. It was like…you know how you get to the end of a really long run and you're craving chips and salsa?"

She laughed quietly. That was a confession she'd made early on. A hard workout left her willing to crawl on hands and knees to gorge on Mexican food.

"It sounds good, but you feel awful afterward if you give in. You have to reload on the stuff your body needs, not necessarily what it wants. Letting Jesus love me, giving Him everything, was like Thanksgiving dinner. I didn't need to go anywhere else. Somehow, I was full. There wasn't room for chips and salsa anymore."

Until now. He'd never craved another human's company so much until now, and it was a craving that only intensified the more he spent time with her.

She eyed him as though she was thinking about something, like she wanted to move but wasn't sure how. "So how do you come to this Thanksgiving dinner kind of place?"

"You give up."

"Give up?"

He felt the joy of his own surrender rising inside him, so fierce he had to smile. Right now, Lucas had to give up, too, to acknowledge he wasn't in charge of Kristin or her future. God was. If God wanted them together, first Kristin had to find God.

"Honestly, Kris, you have to admit you can't do it on your own."

She said nothing, simply studied the underside of the roof like answers might be written there. Finally, she shook her head and pushed to her feet slowly, as though the injuries from the past few days were taking their toll. "I think I need to be alone."

Let her go. He had no choice. She wasn't his responsibility.

Except… "You know I'm bunking on the couch." He wasn't leaving her alone, not until Morrissey was in custody. Too much uncertainty still nagged at the back of his neck. And his gut, the very thing Travis had said he never doubted, said this wasn't over. Something big was about to happen.

Rolling onto her side, Kristin pulled the quilt higher and tucked it under her chin. Few shadows moved in the thin light. Still, too many images vied for her attention, flipping like a deck of cards. The man on the trail and in her kitchen, Specialist Cronin, Brandon Lacey…

Her brother, the money, his motives for coming into her life…

Lucas Murphy…

Jesus.

He was the One Who refused to leave her alone. Lucas had shared his past with her before, told her how he'd treated relationships, how he'd been searching and hurting as he went. Yet, here he was now, unbelievably the man who made her feel safer than any other. If he was telling her the truth about his past, then the only way he could be the man he was today was by some power beyond him.

There was also Hoyt Alston's story, the way Rebecca and the chaplain were both convinced God had intervened.

The way her father had held that knife to her throat yet let her live.

She shut her eyes against the visions, the blood, the horror. She'd managed for years to shove those images into dark places, but lately they sprang up more and more. One horrifying night overarched and shadowed her entire life.

Maybe it was time to stop living like she was the only one who'd ever faced pain and witnessed the worst.

Her self-reliance had been stretched thin these past few days, listening to Lucas and to the soldiers around him. They'd faced blood and horror on a daily basis. Watched friends maimed by faceless attackers, seen life end in nightmarish ways. How did anyone in the military get over what they saw in war? How did Hoyt Alston get over seeing his buddy die in front of him? Being the sole survivor?

Survivor. She sucked in a breath that burned her lungs. Her father had relented at the last second. He'd beaten her, verbally smacked her down, yet he couldn't kill her, even though killing was clearly something he wasn't afraid of.

She'd survived. But for what?

For more than her life right now. All she did was keep busy, working from sunup to sundown, but without purpose. She pushed herself to be strong, pushed others to be strong, all in an attempt to wrestle the past into line, to stay so busy she'd fall into bed at night and sleep without dreaming.

No joy. No fulfillment. No forgiveness.

No surrender.

She was tired. Tired of moving and getting nowhere. That was the very reason she hated running on a treadmill. She preferred the streets, the trails, the change of scenery and the brush of the air on her skin. But her life? One giant treadmill.

For the first time, someone had shown her the head of the trail.

She wasn't sure she dared to forgive her father, dared to let go of the past and stop wrapping it around her like a moldy blanket, tainting everything in her world. Stopped acting as though she had virtue when her father hadn't, as though she, too, didn't need someone to save her.

Her heart beat harder than when Lucas had kissed her, the air so heavy and thick, it felt like a blanket all its own. Warm, like love should feel when it was pure and perfect, not marked by blazing jealousy and white-hot rage. Her parents hadn't had love or even passion. They'd based their marriage on rage. Raging desires. Raging anger.

Kristin had sought the opposite, keeping tight control on her environment and her emotions until she felt nothing at all. Wrapping herself in unforgiveness and deadness instead of pain. Being a dead woman walking wasn't what she'd survived for. Emptiness and nothingness weren't her destiny.

Maybe this was. This thing that felt like overwhelming love.

She wanted it. All of it.

Kristin didn't say a word as she let go. Released her life to the One Who was waiting for her to give up, to open her hand and let Him have her. *Jesus, I don't know much about You, but... I've seen You work. I've been wrong, too, messed everything up. And You're in charge.*

The overwhelming sense of release was almost terrifying. In her whole life, she'd never realized the weight she was dragging until she transferred it to shoulders broader than her own.

She sat bolt upright, chills running along her arms in the best kind of way. She had to tell someone. Had to make this out loud and real.

Lucas. She wanted to tell Lucas, but she also wanted to stay here, wrapped in this blanket of Jesus, real and present.

She leaned against the pillows, reveling in peace. In letting go.

In feeling.

In a rush, the feelings hit hard. She wanted to tell Lucas because she wanted him to know, because he was important. Because yes, she got the same feeling with him that she had right now, but on a whole different level.

She loved Lucas Murphy.

She just didn't know what to do with him.

Life without Lucas was unthinkable. But life with him? After the events of the past week, they could never go back to being the friends they used to be. Kristin wasn't even sure if she wanted that anymore. But she'd never seen a real relationship at work. Had never seen what two people who loved each other unconditionally looked like. Could she love Lucas the way she needed to?

Let go.

If she was letting go of everything else, she could let go of Lucas, too, and let God handle the two of them together.

Surrender. It was harder than she'd thought to be the one not in control.

She slid beneath the quilt and rolled onto her right side, staring at the dark wall, conscious of Lucas downstairs on the couch, almost able to sense his presence.

So different from her father. So different from her brother. In letting go, she could see the truth for the first time. It was clear Kyle had been involved in something horrible, something he'd tangled her in and put her in danger for. Something that led Cronin and Morrissey to believe she was involved.

The truth twisted behind her heart, but not in the stabbing pain she'd feared it would. It came this time with grief for what had never been, not longing for what she could never have.

The more she learned, the more she knew her brother had used her. He'd spent so much time here…but he'd never talked. Never communicated once he left. Came home on his R & R and crashed at her place because he needed a bed to sleep in since he couldn't get into the barracks during a deployment. She'd given, he'd taken.

Except for the basement. He'd worked tirelessly down there before he deployed, finishing the walls and creating a space she'd told him was a dream of hers. Maybe it was his way of showing her love. Maybe it was guilt.

Or maybe…

She sat straight up again, the covers pooling over the thin sweatpants she'd worn to bed.

Or maybe her basement was the answer to everything.

EIGHTEEN

Lucas hefted a hammer and stared at the basement wall. Kristin had told him dozens of times how much she loved her workout space, how it was exactly what she'd always envisioned. The pale green walls made the room lighter and turned it into a place he'd liked lifting weights in when she'd invited him.

Now she wanted to rip everything out in an attempt to get to the bottom of her brother's treachery. So much so that she'd sent him out to the garage at two thirty in the morning for tools and dust masks Kyle had left behind. It wasn't like either of them was sleeping anyway, but still...

"You're sure you want to do this? CID probably has a way they can check behind the walls without physically tearing them out."

Staring at the hammer she held, Kristin surveyed the wall, her eyes grim over the white mask she wore. "I'm sure. I want this over."

"But what makes you think—"

"All along, everybody's been thinking Kyle was in the mail room, sending things out somehow. But where's the evidence? There's been nobody discovered on the receiving end, and everybody thinks Kyle has whatever it is they're after. Cronin may not talk. Nobody knows where Morrissey is. What if we're backward? What if Kyle was the receiver? What if he was tasked with hiding stuff until he found a buyer and then he got killed before he could deliver the goods?"

Lucas dragged his thumb along the hammer's claw. "CID said they were investigating him because of posts he was making on the dark web looking for buyers. Maybe he hid everything and tried to double-cross his partners."

"It doesn't matter. I want this finished. Kyle spent a ton of time here, insistent on putting up drywall and not letting me lift a finger to help. It makes sense he was walling something behind it." She kept her focus on the walls, regret tingeing her expression. "It's not like it can't be fixed. After all, there's ten thousand dollars upstairs, unless the investigators take it. And there's always the insurance money he left me." She curled her lip. "You ready?"

He was more concerned about her readiness. If they ripped the drywall out of this entire room and found nothing, how would she react? And what would it do to the investigation if they couldn't find Kyle's hiding place? Something else nagged at him, too. "Where does his car fit in?"

Kristin approached the wall and rapped a knuckle against the drywall, sounding for a stud to avoid, likely. "I don't know. Revenge?"

"So much of this makes no sense. Back away and think before you do something crazy. There's too many—"

Kristin ended his warning by raring back and smashing a hole into the drywall, embedding the head of the hammer in the wall. "Now we can quit talking." She tilted her head from side to side and pulled the hammer free. "It's actually kind of cathartic." She cocked her arm again, but Lucas grabbed her wrist.

"I'm sure there's something that feels really good right now about smashing walls, but we need a system. You don't want to put a hammer through a two-thousand-year-old vase."

"True." She lowered her arm. "What's the plan?"

"Since you're enjoying the hammer so much, drag the weight bench over and put a row of holes in the top of each piece. I can pull it apart from there."

The pair went to work silently for half an hour, Lucas watching Kristin as she systematically dismantled her dream. Something about her was different. He'd expected her typical hard edge, the emotionless mask he'd seen so many times. Instead, there seemed to be something relaxed about her, something less on edge. And he'd been certain a couple of times he'd seen her swipe at her eyes.

Better not read too much into it. It was probably drywall dust. There hadn't been any goggles in the garage.

"Lucas."

The way she said his name stopped his hands on the piece of drywall he was about to rip out. He let go and stepped up onto the weight bench beside her. "You found something."

"There's no insulation behind this section." Her voice edged with tension, and she aimed the hammer at the holes she'd made in the wall. "Those all had solid insulation behind them. The minute I hammered into this one, it's hollow." She made another series of holes, and together they pulled apart the drywall, revealing several packages wrapped in everything from newspapers to towels to T-shirts.

Kristin gasped and stepped off the weight bench as though the packages were radioactive, staring at the sight. Her face blanched. "Lucas. I can't…"

Shoving the dust mask off his head, Lucas jumped down to join her, but he kept his distance. She needed space, needed to process what he was beginning to see.

Her breathing came rapidly as her eyes welled with tears. "He did everything they said he did. He did it and he used me and my house and he put me in danger. He pretended to be doing me a favor." She aimed a finger at the wall, rocked more than any physical attack over the past few days had hit her. "These things are important to the Iraqi people, to their culture and their history, and my brother…" Her voice was muffled by the dust mask that still covered her mouth. "They're in my walls. I'm living in a movie."

She turned toward him and, for the first time, reached for him first.

Something hitched in Lucas's chest. She needed him. Gently, he slipped the dust mask over her head then pulled her closer. She didn't cry, but she drew support from him. He'd held her before, but never had she let him do the comforting. It felt…right.

"I'm sorry." Her voice muffled into his shoulder, and she straightened, swiping a dusty finger beneath her eye and leaving a streak of gray behind. "My head won't wrap around this. It's unreal. There's art and history stolen from a country and it's in my wall." Kristin turned away, staring at the gaping hole they'd ripped away. "And my brother is the bad guy."

"I know." Lucas wanted to pull her closer again, but he stopped himself. Right now, he had to act from his mind, not from his heart. "I have to call CID and tell them what we found."

"I know."

Did she really? "They'll question you. May rip the rest of your house apart."

"Lucas. I know." Her voice was resigned, heavier than the hammers they'd wielded in their search. She rolled her eyes toward the ceiling. "You make the call. I'm going upstairs for some water." Without lifting her head, she trudged up the stairs, her shoulders slack, defeat he'd never seen before pulling her low.

Lucas watched her go, torn between following her or doing what he knew he had to do…officially making her brother a bad guy, one of the toughest calls he'd ever had to make. He'd been a pain, but Kyle Coleman had also been one of his soldiers.

Before he could even reach for his phone, it vibrated in his hip pocket. He checked the screen, adrenaline surging. Travis.

Clearing his throat, he pulled the phone to his ear. "I don't know why you're calling, but Kristin and I found her brother's stash."

There was a long silence before Travis inhaled audibly. "I hate to tell you, but we've got worse news to deal with."

Please, no. Lucas couldn't handle more problems. All he wanted was to get CID to the house and get it cleared so Kristin's life could go back to normal. More complications weren't on the agenda. "What?"

"Cronin isn't as deeply involved as we thought. He

was blackmailed by Morrissey to pull surveillance on Brandon Lacey."

"Makes sense if Lacey was—"

"Specialist Lacey wasn't involved."

Lucas sank to the weight bench and dropped his head. If Lacey wasn't involved, then either they had two killers in the unit, or the kid had died an innocent bystander.

"Wrong place, wrong time. Cronin said Morrissey started out asking him to keep tabs on Lacey after Kristin delivered the package to him on post. He thought Kristin's brother had turned on him and was working with Lacey. Morrissey killed Lacey because he thought Lacey had the goods."

"Lacey was innocent." Lucas was going to be sick. All he could see was Brandon Lacey's slightly gangly, always awkward self, the goofy kid who'd morphed into a competent soldier every single time his platoon needed him. Now it looked as though his death was even more pointless than they'd thought.

Somebody had to stop William Morrissey. He'd already crossed the line from threats to murder. There was no going back now, and that put Kristin in even deeper danger. "Any word on where Morrissey is?"

"I got very little out of CID. But, Lucas, watch your back. He's getting desperate. At this point, if he thinks Kristin knows anything, he's not going to play games."

"Why?" Kristin gripped the edge of the sink, the stainless steel beneath her fingers a cool contrast to her heated prayer. It was awkward, voicing the pain in her heart to Someone she couldn't see or hear. She shut her eyes and tightened her hold on the counter. Surrender.

It hadn't bought her anything. She'd given everything up, and things should have gotten better. Shouldn't Kyle have been innocent? Shouldn't things have changed?

Dropping her head, she waited for the peace she'd felt earlier. Instead of a blanket, though, she found tattered edges.

It was still more than she'd had before. It was enough.

Kristin dug for rational thought. Her surrender would only help her. It couldn't magically erase the past, undo history and make her brother a good person. Surrender affected her, not Kyle or Lucas or anyone else.

A sudden pain squeezed inside her chest, robbing her lungs of air. What had happened to Kyle? He was dead, his second chances all gone.

On top of everything else, not this. Not now. She gulped air and regretted the glass of water she'd downed. Regretted ever eating anything in her whole life.

Fresh air. She needed to get outside and into air lighter than the heaviness in her kitchen. Pushing for the door, she frantically pressed the buttons on the alarm keypad and burst out onto the porch, heaving air like she'd been drowning.

She had to focus on what was right in front of her. All she had was right now, and she could deal with right now.

Right now, there were valuable pieces hidden in her basement walls. She didn't have to unwrap the packages to know what they were. The evidence said it all. Art and historical pieces valuable to an entire nation were hidden in her house. Kristin almost wanted to laugh at the absurdity. Not a lot of people could lay claim to that. History had never interested her, but part of her wanted to at least touch something, to be able to say she had.

She dragged her hands through her hair. Okay, she was losing reality here. Lucas would call CID and report what they'd uncovered. She'd face questions, but she'd done nothing wrong, so there was nothing to fear. And once William Morrissey and whoever else had come after her heard the goods were no longer in her possession, well, this would be over.

Over.

She could have her life back. Could stop looking over her shoulder.

Could tell Lucas she was falling in love with him.

This was either the beginning of a whole new thing in her life or the ending of a friendship she'd come to value more than any other, one that challenged her, pierced her soul and changed her life. Once she confessed everything to Lucas, she'd change their friendship forever. Either into something she'd never known she craved or into ashes. After she'd shoved him away constantly and acted like he was a criminal after he kissed her, she wouldn't fault him if he ran as far as he could to get away from her.

Lord, give me a chance to explain.

It was coming easier, this praying thing.

She stared across the yard at the empty garage and said another quick prayer for the Camaro's return. It was all she had left of her brother and, even though he'd proved to be the worst of what everyone thought, he was still the only family she'd had left.

Kristin stretched out the side of her neck and turned to head to the basement to wait for CID with Lucas. Maybe even to talk to him about what would happen next between them.

A movement from the deck stairs turned her head,

and a body slammed into her, knocking her to the wide wooden boards below and blasting the breath from her lungs. She gasped and fought the weight that pinned her on her side, shoulder digging painfully into the rough deck board. She tried to see out of her peripheral who her attacker was, but she already knew it had to be William Morrissey.

Fighting a rising panic, she grasped at what she knew. She'd successfully fought him off in the woods, though she'd failed in her kitchen. She was batting .500. Well, that was good enough.

Slackening her shoulder, she gained enough leverage to roll onto her back, freeing her hand and driving it toward Morrissey's chin. The blow glanced at an angle, and he grunted, leaning away then regrouping fast, slamming something cold and hard against her forehead.

Kristin froze. A pistol. Hard and cold and bruising... pressed to her head.

NINETEEN

Lucas pressed End on the phone and stared at the screen. This couldn't get much worse.

"Lucas?"

He lifted his head and felt a rush of cold fear. Kristin stood at the top of the stairs, a figure behind her holding the barrel of a pistol to the side of her head.

Her face was white, the lines around her mouth tight as her eyes locked on Lucas.

His body stiffened, and he rocketed to his feet, scanning for anything he could use as a weapon. He jerked a hammer from the weight bench and gripped it hard, his fingers aching with the strain. It was all he had. All he had against a gunman with Kristin helpless.

Her worst nightmare.

And now his.

A man's voice spoke, and Kristin eased down two stairs as her captor stepped into view behind her.

William Morrissey, his dark eyes trained on Lucas. Gone was the man who'd fought by Lucas's side overseas, the man whom everyone had believed to be a top-notch soldier. Lucas's thoughts folded over on themselves, fighting to reconcile this new reality with his past. He kneaded the hammer in his fist, trying to find a way to get Kristin out of danger. Morrissey didn't want her. He was after what was hidden in her basement walls. "Let her go and I'll help you get this stuff out of here."

"I let her go, I have no leverage. You'll get the stuff out of here to the truck, then we'll talk." His voice was hard and matter-of-fact, the voice of a man who'd do anything to get what he wanted. He'd already killed his own platoon mate. He wouldn't hesitate to take Kristin out, too. "Put down the hammer."

Lucas cut his eyes to Kristin, who caught his and never turned away, cold panic shifting across her features. The gun at her head had her frozen, the danger likely recalling the worst night of her life.

He set the hammer on the bench, watching Kristin the whole time, trying to ground her in this space, in his presence. In the fact she could trust him.

In the fact she could save herself if she could snap out of this.

He flicked his gaze to the side, away from the gun to Morrissey behind her.

Kristin didn't move; her expression didn't change.

Hours passed in the next seconds as Lucas tried to communicate with her as Morrissey watched.

"Enough." He urged Kristin farther down the stairs, keeping the weapon leveled to the side of her head, his finger on the trigger guard but not yet in firing position.

That was all Lucas needed for now. Kristin wasn't hearing him, but if he played this right, maybe he could get Morrissey close enough to disarm him. Or to get through to Kristin. "Tell me what to do and we'll get this over with." He didn't trust the other man one bit, knew if he held to past experience, he'd kill them both as soon as they weren't useful anymore. Kristin was alive now because she was the pawn in this game, the pawn to keep Lucas moving. Once they were done…

Lucas cast a glance at Kristin and tried again. If she heard him, the move was dangerous, but it might be all they had. "You know, you're brave getting close to her. She tore Cronin apart at the company today."

Something flashed in Kristin's expression, but then she swayed and grabbed the stair's open railing, trying to steady herself.

Morrissey chuckled. "He was too easy on her. If he'd been rougher, she'd have talked sooner and we wouldn't be here now. He should have—"

His words sliced off as Kristin braced herself against the railing and threw her head backward, connecting with Morrissey's nose and driving him against the wall.

The gun fell from his hand and bounced off the corner of one of the open stairs before clattering to the cement floor and disappearing beneath the staircase.

Lucas dived for the weapon as the stairs above him shook and thudded, but it had disappeared into the shadows. He couldn't search long. Kristin needed him. He came to his feet in time to see her land a solid blow to Morrissey's bleeding nose before he roared and shoved her away.

She staggered down three steps but kept her balance as she skittered backward across the floor. She caught her footing and charged.

"Kristin, don't!" Lucas lunged toward them. She didn't need to get in reach of the man again. If he got a hand on her before Lucas could dive in…

But the words weren't even out of his mouth before

a shot cracked and a bullet slammed into the floor at Kristin's feet.

Morrissey had a second weapon.

Lucas skidded to a stop a few feet from Kristin as she froze.

"Now that I have your attention." Morrissey kept the gun leveled at Kristin, pain deepening the lines around his eyes as blood streamed from his nose and darkened the front of his black shirt. "Both of you are alive right now because I need you to do the heavy lifting while I keep an eye on her. But, trust me, I won't hesitate to tear this place apart myself if I have to."

"I don't know where Kyle hid anything." Kristin's voice was low, her head still turned toward the gun in Morrissey's hand.

Lucas couldn't tell if she was frozen in place or faking weak to make a play. From his angle slightly behind her, he couldn't see her face.

"Looks like you dug some out already, so I'm guessing you know where the rest is, too." Morrissey turned to Lucas. "She offered you a cut? Never figured you'd go dirty."

"I didn't. CID will get everything we've found."

The blow landed. As Morrissey's fingers tightened around the pistol's grip, something like panic flashed across his face, but then he strengthened his stance. "I don't think so. I have to turn it over to some men who aren't too happy it's taken this long to get a delivery."

Lucas's eyes narrowed. The way he was talking, William Morrissey wasn't the head of this operation like everybody thought. "You're a courier, like Coleman was."

Morrissey's eye twitched, and he jerked the gun toward the open wall. "Start packing that into boxes."

"You didn't kill him, did you?" Lucas eased closer to his former soldier, everything coming into focus. If Morrissey had killed Coleman, he wouldn't have hesitated to kill Kristin. He wasn't a mastermind. He was a punk running scared. "You made certain you came up hot on the drug test. You wanted out of the country, to come here, where it was safe. Who's after you?"

Without turning away from Lucas, Morrissey whipped the gun to Kristin, his arm steady. "No more questions."

"You know, if you didn't kill Kyle, then—"

"I said get moving!" The roar of his voice blended with the thunder of the pistol firing.

Lucas's whole body froze, air trapped in his lungs as Kristin dropped to her knees, blood staining the left shoulder of her teal workout shirt. Her eyes locked with his, wide with pain and confusion.

Lucas scrambled to Kristin, pulling his sweatshirt over his head as he banged his knees on the floor. He eased her to lean against the wall and assessed the damage before pressing his sweatshirt tight to her shoulder, trying to get a rein on his anger and fear before they swamped him and dulled his tactical thinking. He had to turn away from her, to find a way to take out William Morrissey before he fired again.

"Back away from her, Sarge. We get moving. Now."

Lucas ignored him. "Stay with me." He grabbed Kristin's right hand and pressed it against the sweatshirt over her wound. "I'll get us out of this."

She met him with a hard stare, then shifted her gaze to the right, to the floor beneath the stairs, her expression a silent signal.

Easing back as though he were going to stand, Lucas followed her signal and caught a glint of the pistol Morrissey had dropped earlier, lying near Kristin's foot, out of his reach.

But not out of hers.

Standing, Lucas eased away from Kristin, lifting his hands in mock surrender. "Tell me what to load the stuff in, but don't hurt her again."

Morrissey nodded and jerked his chin toward the far corner of the basement. "Those plastic bins over there. Use them."

Edging toward the open space between Kristin and the stairs, Lucas nodded. "I'll do that." He glanced at Kristin. They had exactly one chance to either end this thing or die trying. He swallowed hard. Everything hinged on the next five seconds. "Now."

Sweeping her leg, Kristin kicked the pistol from beneath the stair and sent it skittering toward Lucas, who was already diving for it. His fingers closed around the grip as he rolled to one knee, took aim and pulled the trigger.

TWENTY

Kristin eased into the couch cushions and hurled an orange at the front door. The entire world was frustrating.

"Was that really necessary?" Casey bent and retrieved the bruised fruit. "What did vitamin C ever do to you?"

"I can't even peel an orange." Kristin threw her good hand into the air. Her whole body ached, but her shoulder and back led the charge with searing, throbbing pain even prescription ibuprofen hadn't dulled. The doctor had ordered more powerful pain medication, but she didn't want to touch it. It made her woozy, and woozy was worse than pain any day. The bullet through her shoulder had required surgery, but she wouldn't believe everything was going to heal properly until she felt the proof. "I hate sitting still."

"You hate being helpless, you mean." Dropping onto the couch beside Kristin, Casey peeled the orange and passed over a section. "Good news is you can't stress eat yourself into a vitamin C overdose. At least not without some help."

"You're such an optimist."

"And you're such a crank."

"I'm not cranky."

"Yes, you are. As cranky as a two-year-old who's an hour late for nap time." Casey sectioned the rest of the orange and spread it on a paper towel on the coffee table. "Somehow, I think this is less about pain and more about the fact Lucas isn't at your bedside anymore."

Kristin bit her tongue before she protested too much. Lucas had been by her side in the hospital but had gone to work this morning to deal with the fallout from Morrissey's treachery and the shooting that had left him wounded but recovering.

"Any word about who was behind everything? Who killed your brother and was pulling Morrissey's strings?"

"No." Kristin shook her head. "I asked Lucas to run point between me and the cops but…" No news. No word.

And no time alone with him. Doctors and nurses had been in and out at the hospital, and Casey had hardly left her side. When would she get to tell him what had happened in her heart before William Morrissey almost destroyed everything?

She couldn't rewind to what they'd had before. And after the way he'd kissed her, she was pretty sure he felt the same.

Two taps on the door sent her heart rate so high she was glad the heart monitor at the hospital was no longer in play.

Lucas slipped through the door, his brown eyes sparking with something that swirled in her stomach in the best of ways. "Doing any better than you were this morning?" He swept his beret from his head and shut the door behind him.

It took a second for Kristin to find her voice. Now

that she'd opened her heart, she always had to prepare herself to see him. "I was fine this morning."

"Wrong." Casey stood and swiped her hands down her jeans as she looked at Lucas. "You going to be here for a while? I have to go in to the office."

"I don't need a nurse."

"Yeah, I'll hang around." Lucas winked at Kristin, and her last protest died as Casey slipped into her jacket and out the door without another word.

Kristin winced and watched her go. Clearly, she was taxing enough to send her best friend packing at the first opportunity. "Am I that difficult?"

Lucas threw his jacket over the back of the chair and eased onto the couch beside her, careful not to jostle her shoulder. "Let's say it's a good thing I know who you really are when the pain isn't talking."

"Sorry."

"No worries. I can handle you." He smiled, and Kristin's stomach quivered. "They found the Camaro."

It took a second for the shift in his conversation to register. She turned so fast the muscles in her shoulder protested. "Seriously?"

"Safe and sound in a storage unit on Yadkin Road."

Kristin felt her shoulders ease, some of the tension peeling away with the news. Kyle might have done her wrong, but she still needed a piece of family to help the grief heal. "Who took it?"

Lucas stretched his arms along the back of the sofa, letting his fingers rest in her hair and brush against her neck, sending a warm shudder through her that made her forget all about the pain. "Guy named Arlo Henshaw is the ringleader. He's been at this for two decades, hitting war-torn countries and selling their antiquities to the highest bidder. And, believe me, there are some high bidders. He dangles cash in front of young soldiers, convinces them these treasures are better off in the hands of people who will care for them and get them out of harm's way. He's smooth."

"And Kyle bought into it?"

His fingers stilled, then moved in slow circles in the hair at the nape of her neck. "So, the car… After Kyle was killed, Morrissey decided to take his place. He failed his drug test on purpose, hoping we'd send him here so he could retrieve what Kyle hid, but he didn't count on us holding him until we redeployed and then confining him to quarters until he chaptered out. He tried to break in the day after he got out, but it set off your alarm, so he came at you on the trail thinking you were working with Kyle and would talk. When you didn't, he took your keys and was going to use the clicker on your key ring…"

"But I had the remotes for the alarm disabled."

"He set off the alarm again, and he didn't want anyone to know he'd been here, so he had to make it seem like a simple robbery. The car key was by the back door and the Camaro was collateral damage."

Kristin fingered the edge of her sweatshirt, her eyes following the motion of her hands while her gut sank lower, along with her voice. She didn't want to ask the question, but she had to know. "Who killed Kyle?"

Lucas slipped his hand from her neck and laced his fingers through hers. It was almost enough to make her forget everything else. "Kyle was the receiver. They shipped the things here to him, and he hid them until they found a buyer. The ten grand was a payment before he came home on R & R. He'd have gotten the second half when he delivered, but he never delivered."

"Greed?"

His fingers tightened around hers. "A bigger payday. He stole from Arlo Henshaw. He was supposed to ship a bunch of the items after we redeployed, but instead, he'd been on the dark web getting buyers of his own. When he didn't ship out orders on R & R like he was supposed to, Henshaw had Morrissey kill him." He let go of her hand and laid a finger on her cheek, turning her to face him. "He knew it was risky and they'd come after him, and I'm guessing that's why he willed the car to you while he was home on R & R, why he made you his beneficiary on his insurance. Some part of him wanted to take care of you."

She turned away, a sense of peace beyond description washing over the grief that tried to set in. Sure, he'd done a lot she would never be able to explain, but Kyle had tried to reach out to her in the end, even if he'd inadvertently pointed the finger of suspicion at her. She'd survived.

Lucas had insisted once that Kristin had "survived for a reason." Maybe it had been for this, to bring a killer to justice. Or maybe... She turned her head, muscles trembling with the weight of what she was about to do, and eyed Lucas, who was watching her with concern. "Maybe it's you."

His expression darkened, the skepticism heavy. "Maybe it's me what?"

"I'm here for a reason. You said it yourself." Baring her soul was harder than she'd thought it would be, even to the man who'd unlocked the door in the first place. "The other night, before we tore apart the basement,

I had a long talk with Jesus. There's a reason I'm still here. Maybe the reason, or part of it, is…"

"Me?"

"Maybe." She held her breath, watching him carefully. She'd laid herself out there, told him everything on her heart. Would he want what she was offering?

His eyes searched hers as a slow smile lifted the corner of his mouth. "Maybe?" His voice was husky, and his gaze wandered to her lips before coming back up. "There's no maybe." He trailed a finger down her cheek. "I can't be happy with what we had last week or last month. I either walk away right now or I kiss you. And if I kiss you, that's it. There's no going back. Because if you want the truth, Kristin James…" His finger drifted across her lower lip, a caress with as much promise as any kiss. "I already know I'm in love with you."

The breath caught in Kristin's throat, and the jolt erased the pain in her shoulder. It erased everything except Lucas. She smiled, then closed the space between them, sealing her answer in the kiss…and in her heart.

EPILOGUE

Kristin reached the finish line with a quick glance at her time, then propped her hands on her hips and walked, throwing a half wave to the small crowd gathered to cheer on the runners at the end. She wrinkled her nose. It wasn't her best time for a half marathon, and it wasn't the marathon she'd been training with Lucas for when everything blew up in March, but considering she'd had a rough comeback from the shooting, she'd take it.

And she'd still beaten Lucas.

He caught up to her, nudging her with his shoulder. "Don't gloat. It was only seven seconds."

"An eternity in running time."

"Feeling okay?"

She grinned sideways at him. Better than okay. The October morning was perfect for running. Lucas had been by her side the whole way until he'd challenged her for a sprint to the finish...which she'd won. After months of physical therapy and training, her shoulder hardly ached at all.

But she knew the question ran deeper. Today marked a goal in her heart, too. Finishing this half marathon had been the prize she'd kept her eye on through all of the physical pain the past few months, but it had pushed her through the emotional, too. Grieving her brother and coming to grips with his thievery.

She'd stopped halfway through training runs more times than she cared to admit, the physical pain drawing the emotional to the surface. Every single time, Lucas had been right there, holding her up, making her fall more in love with him than she'd ever thought she was capable of.

Always pointing her closer to the Savior Who loved her more.

"Kris? You going to answer?"

She accepted an orange from the race volunteer who was handing them out at the end of the gauntlet of supporters. "What do you think?"

Grasping her hand, Lucas pulled her sideways out of the line of runners still trickling in. He wrapped his arms around her and pulled her close, pressing his forehead to hers. "I think you're always going to be snarky."

"Probably." The word broke. Seven months, and he still had the power to steal her breath, especially after she'd barely caught it again.

"I'm proud of you." His voice lowered, and he backed away, letting his eyes drift to her lips and back up again.

"Yeah, well…" Kristin tried to pull away, to cover the embarrassment she always felt when he said stuff like that, stuff she still wasn't used to hearing.

He didn't let her go. "So, I think you're ready now."

"To start training for a marathon?"

The teasing spark in his eye flamed into something entirely different, and his arms tightened around her. "No."

"For what?" Something about the way he was looking about her, about the way he held her close in spite of the crowd around them, fluttered in her stomach and shot adrenaline through her system, stealing her voice until it came out in a faint whisper.

"I hadn't planned to do this until tonight, but…" He slipped a loose curl behind her ear and let his finger trail down her cheek to her neck, leaving warmth in its wake. "You're ready to hear me ask you to marry me."

His declaration caught her right in the knees. If his arms hadn't been around her, she'd have probably struggled to stay on her feet. She hadn't heard him right. Her mouth opened, closed, and she couldn't look away from his eyes, watching hers.

A slow smile tipped the corners of his mouth. "Since you usually have no problem arguing loudly when you disagree with me, I'm going to be optimistic and say silence means you agree." He leaned closer, his whisper a breath against her lips. "Nod if I'm right."

Kristin swallowed hard and nodded once, then laced her fingers behind his neck and pulled him closer, losing herself in his kiss…and in the freedom of surrender.

* * * * *

If you enjoyed DEAD RUN, look for these other military suspense books from Jodie Bailey:

FREEFALL
CROSSFIRE
SMOKESCREEN
COMPROMISED IDENTITY
BREACH OF TRUST

Dear Reader,

First off, I would like to say that my brother is nothing like Kyle Coleman.

This book was a little bit different than any other suspense, because I usually start with a crime and then build in characters and their faith. This time, Kristin came along and demanded to be put in a story. Of course she did. Would you expect her to do anything different? I knew she'd had pain. I knew her life had been tragic.

And I knew her brother was not the good guy who only looked guilty.

That was tough. What do we do when people aren't who we thought they were? When we have to face that there is fault in all of us, even in the people we love? Kristin had to face those questions head-on. Why? Because we all have to face them at some point. And it is our relationship with our Savior that determines whether we face those moments with grace or with devastation.

Me? I don't know where I'd be without Jesus. And like Kristin, I find surrender hard. Every day I find it hard. I like to do things my own way, to take care of things myself. Is anybody else nodding their head right now, or is it just me?

The one thing I've found is this… Surrender doesn't mean life becomes this giant la-la happy land of roses. But it does make the hard days easier. I meant when I said I don't know where I'd be without Jesus. Because when I look back on the hard times, I don't see pain. I see Him. I see the people He placed in my life. I feel

His presence. And I know I never was alone, not even for one moment.

The very thing that Kristin had to learn.

And I feel compelled to ask… Are you there yet?

Thank you so much for running the race with Kristin and Lucas. (Fun story about Lucas—that wasn't his name at first. But when I tried to type his story with his original name, he refused to show up on the page. Kept insisting he was Lucas and refusing to talk. Stubborn man.) I hope you'll stop by and visit me at www.jodiebailey.com or, if you're curious to see if the pictures in your head match the pictures in mine, you'll drop by Pinterest and check out the story boards there. And I always love to hear from you at Jodie@jodiebailey.com.

Thanks again for reading. I'm honored.

Jodie Bailey

COMING NEXT MONTH FROM
Love Inspired® Suspense

Available February 7, 2017

THE ONLY WITNESS
Callahan Confidential • by Laura Scott
Paige Olson's five-year-old daughter may have witnessed her father's murder, but she won't talk about it—and now a gunman's hunting them down. Homicide detective Miles Callahan will do anything to protect Paige and her little girl...even if it means breaking police protocol.

SHADOW OF SUSPICION • by Christy Barritt
Framed for kidnapping her neighbor's daughter, computer specialist Laney Ryan needs help to prove her innocence. But as she and police detective Mark James dig into the case, they become the targets of an unknown threat.

DESERT SECRETS • by Lisa Harris
Kidnapped and tormented into revealing the location of her brother—and the money he stole—Lexi Shannon's convinced she'll be killed...until pilot Colton Landry comes to her rescue. But after their plane's shot down as they attempt to escape, they're thrust into a deadly desert pursuit.

RESCUE AT CEDAR LAKE
True North Bodyguards • by Maggie K. Black
When Theresa Vaughan is attacked at a remote snowbound cottage by a masked man seeking a secret from her past, her only hope of survival is Alex Dean, the daring bodyguard whose heart she broke when she ended their engagement.

PERILOUS HOMECOMING • by Sarah Varland
As the sole witness to a murder, Kelsey Jackson finds herself in a killer's crosshairs. But with the help of her high school rival, Sawyer Hamilton, she's determined to catch the murderer before she becomes the next victim.

PRESUMED DEAD • by Angela Ruth Strong
Preston Tyler's supposed to be dead...so Holly Fontaine can't believe the former soldier just rescued her from a bomb planted in her cabin. And with a killer after her, the childhood sweetheart she believed was gone forever is the only man who can save her.

LOOK FOR THESE AND OTHER LOVE INSPIRED BOOKS WHEREVER BOOKS ARE SOLD, INCLUDING MOST BOOKSTORES, SUPERMARKETS, DISCOUNT STORES AND DRUGSTORES.

LISCNM0117

REQUEST YOUR FREE BOOKS!

2 FREE INSPIRATIONAL NOVELS
PLUS 2
FREE
MYSTERY GIFTS

Love Inspired®

YES! Please send me 2 FREE Love Inspired® novels and my 2 FREE mystery gifts (gifts are worth about $10). After receiving them, if I don't wish to receive any more books, I can return the shipping statement marked "cancel." If I don't cancel, I will receive 6 brand-new novels every month and be billed just $4.99 per book in the U.S. or $5.49 per book in Canada. That's a saving of at least 17% off the cover price. It's quite a bargain! Shipping and handling is just 50¢ per book in the U.S. and 75¢ per book in Canada.* I understand that accepting the 2 free books and gifts places me under no obligation to buy anything. I can always return a shipment and cancel at any time. Even if I never buy another book, the two free books and gifts are mine to keep forever.

105/305 IDN GH5P

Name _____ (PLEASE PRINT) _____

Address _____ Apt. # _____

City _____ State/Prov. _____ Zip/Postal Code _____

Signature (if under 18, a parent or guardian must sign)

Mail to the **Reader Service:**
IN U.S.A.: P.O. Box 1867, Buffalo, NY 14240-1867
IN CANADA: P.O. Box 609, Fort Erie, Ontario L2A 5X3

**Are you a subscriber to Love Inspired® books
and want to receive the larger-print edition?
Call 1-800-873-8635 or visit www.ReaderService.com.**

* Terms and prices subject to change without notice. Prices do not include applicable taxes. Sales tax applicable in N.Y. Canadian residents will be charged applicable taxes. Offer not valid in Quebec. This offer is limited to one order per household. Not valid for current subscribers to Love Inspired books. All orders subject to credit approval. Credit or debit balances in a customer's account(s) may be offset by any other outstanding balance owed by or to the customer. Please allow 4 to 6 weeks for delivery. Offer available while quantities last.

Your Privacy—The Reader Service is committed to protecting your privacy. Our Privacy Policy is available online at www.ReaderService.com or upon request from the Reader Service.

We make a portion of our mailing list available to reputable third parties that offer products we believe may interest you. If you prefer that we not exchange your name with third parties, or if you wish to clarify or modify your communication preferences, please visit us at www.ReaderService.com/consumerschoice or write to us at Reader Service Preference Service, P.O. Box 9062, Buffalo, NY 14240-9062. Include your complete name and address.

LII5

SPECIAL EXCERPT FROM

SUSPENSE

*Paige Olson's five-year-old daughter may have
witnessed her father's murder, but she won't talk
about it—and now a gunman's hunting them down.
Homicide detective Miles Callahan will do anything
to protect Paige and her little girl...even if it means
breaking police protocol.*

Read on for a sneak preview of
THE ONLY WITNESS
*by **Laura Scott**, available February 2017
from Love Inspired Suspense!*

"I looked up the license plate of the black sedan from the restaurant," Miles said, his expression grim. "The sedan is registered to Sci-Tech."

"They sent gunmen after us?" Paige asked in a strained whisper.

"Yeah, that's what it looks like."

"They're after me because of my ex-husband, aren't they?"

"I think so, yes." Miles reached over and cradled her icy hands in his. "I'm sorry."

Paige gripped his hands tightly. "You have to find Travis before it's too late."

He didn't want to point out that it might already be too late. Whatever Abby had seen on the tablet had frightened her to the point she wouldn't speak. Had Travis told her to keep quiet? Or had she seen something horrible? He found himself hoping for the first option, but feared the latter.

LISEXP0117

"I'm not sure where to look for Travis," he admitted. "There's no way to know where he'd go to hide if he thought he was in danger."

"Did you give the police the list of names I gave you?" Paige asked. "I know they're only a few names, but…"

"I've been searching on their names, but I haven't found anything yet. At least we have another link to Sci-Tech. No wonder they were stonewalling me."

"I might be able to get inside the building," Paige offered.

"No." His knee-jerk reaction surprised him, and he tried to backpedal. "I mean, if they're the ones behind this, then it's not safe for you to go there. Besides, how would you get in?"

She lifted her uncertain gaze to his. "I know a couple of the security guards pretty well. If I waited until after-hours, when there's only one security guard manning the desk, I might be able to convince them to let me in."

"I know you want to help, but it's not worth the risk." He couldn't stand the idea of Paige walking into the equivalent of the lion's den. "You don't know for sure which security guard would be on duty. And besides, if anything happened—Abby would be lost without you."

She blinked, and he thought he saw the glint of tears. "Logically, I know you're right, but it's hard to sit back and do nothing, not even trying."

"I'll find a way to do something while keeping you and Abby safe." He couldn't stand the thought of her worrying about things she couldn't change. He'd protect her, no matter what.

Don't miss
THE ONLY WITNESS
by Laura Scott, available February 2017 wherever
Love Inspired® Suspense books and ebooks are sold.

www.LoveInspired.com

LISEXP0117

Turn your love of reading into rewards you'll love with

Harlequin My Rewards

Join for FREE today at
www.HarlequinMyRewards.com

Earn **FREE BOOKS** of your choice.

Experience **EXCLUSIVE OFFERS** and contests.

Enjoy **BOOK RECOMMENDATIONS**
selected just for you.

PLUS! Sign up now
and get **500** points
right away!

Earn
FREE
REWARDS
HarlequinMyRewards.com
Join
Today!

MYR16R